Wrong Time, Wrong Place

Lesley Choyce

Formac Publishing Limited,
Halifax, Nova Scotia 1991

© Lesley Choyce 1991

Cover illustration: Mike Little

Canadian Cataloguing in Publication Data

Choyce, Lesley, 1951–
    Wrong time, wrong place

ISBN 0–88780–340–7(pbk)
ISBN 0–88780–099–8(bound)

I. Title.

PS8555.H668W76 1995   jC813'.54   C95–950288-2
PZ7.C46Wr   1995

Formac Publishing Company Limited
5502 Atlantic Street
Halifax, N.S. B3H 1G4

Printed and bound in Canada

Contents

1	Where There's Smoke	1
2	Foot-ankle Express to Nowhere	4
3	Larry	10
4	The Biggest Problem in the World	14
5	Blood Red	19
6	Heartless Keeps the Lid on	24
7	The Mirror Must Be Lying	30
8	Bad News Laundromat	35
9	Shakespeare's Revenge	41
10	Stuck with Trouble	47
11	Rattletrap, Reeds and Tin Man	50
12	One Good Move	54
13	Africville Ghost Town	59
14	Just the Way Things Are	64
15	The Invisible Man	69
16	The Same Old Trap	73
17	Seeing It Through	77
18	On the Run	82
19	A Million Miles from Home	84
20	Confronting the Truth	89
21	Back Over the Line	93
22	The "R" Word	99
23	Driving Lesson	106
24	Mirror, Mirror …	112

Chapter One

Where There's Smoke

What happened at school was not my fault. Unfortunately, there was no one to blame but me so I was guilty. Doesn't matter what the truth is.

This is the way it really went. Denise and I had been arguing for a couple of weeks. She got into this new image thing — very hip and very black. And I guess she just decided that I didn't fit into her life. She wanted a guy more like Harris. So we started arguing there in the hallway. She told me it was over. I guess I should have seen this coming a long way off. But when she said the words, it was as if she had just taken a knife and twisted it around in my guts.

I felt like hitting somebody or kicking in the glass on the big trophy case there in the hall. But I didn't do a thing. I sure didn't feel like going to sit in Harlow's English class and listen to him droning on about Shakespeare. So I went into the lavatory and sat down on the ledge by the window. The place was full of smoke. I think half the guys in the school had been in there puffing on cigarettes between classes. But now I was alone and that's the way I wanted it.

The smoke was thick so I tried to open the window. That's when Coach Jencks walked into the place. He took one look at me and one look at the stomped out

1

cigarette butts on the floor and decided that he had just caught the most serious chain smoker at Thompson High.

"You don't ever seem to learn do you, Wheeler?" he said. Guilty as charged. "Let's go see Mr. Hartman."

I didn't even try to defend myself. What was the point? Heartless Hartman, the principal, told me I was in trouble, big trouble.

"Smell my breath," I said. "I haven't been smoking."

"Good trick, Wheeler. But if you think I'm gonna lean over and breathe in your foul cigarette stench, you're crazy. You'd think that would be pretty funny, I suppose."

"I just want you to see that I haven't smoked anything."

"I caught him red-handed," Mr Jencks said. "I walked in as he was opening the window to let the smoke out."

Hartman called my mother to come into the school. She was upset but very polite around Hartman. I couldn't stand the way she treated him like an important person. She kept apologizing to him and looking at me with disappointment. But what I hated worst was the way Hartman talked to her. I can't quite describe it but I had this feeling that Hartman wouldn't talk to all the parents this way. He was talking down to her, as if all he saw in front of him was an uneducated, unimportant black woman.

It made me mad. I wanted to tell that creep that my mother was going to university. I wanted to tell him just what kind of a woman my mother is. But I just kept my mouth shut.

At home, my mother asked me what happened. I told her about Denise dumping me for Harris, but I didn't try to explain why. And she believed me when I told her that I wasn't smoking in the lavatory. My father wasn't quite so forgiving.

"Corey," he said, "you just don't seem to learn. You have to be more careful. Hartman's got it in for you. Don't do anything that looks remotely like trouble. Just do what you're supposed to and play it by the rules. And be more careful who you hang out with. You know, people judge you by the company you keep."

What he meant was, stop hanging out with Dean and Harris, and start hanging out with more white kids. Sometimes I wonder how a white guy like my old man could have ended up with my mom.

Chapter Two

Foot-ankle Express to Nowhere

I holed up in my room for the evening to try and avoid my old man's lectures and my mom's sad looks. Unfortunately, the lectures and the sadness greeted me at breakfast. By the time I had finished eating, I figured I had already put up with enough hassles for one day. There was no way I could face up to another day of putting in time at Thompson High waiting for the axe to fall down on my head. I couldn't handle another confrontation with Hartman, so I decided to cut school and go across the harbour to Halifax. I'd just walk around in Scotia Square or downtown. Maybe nobody would miss me. Besides, I was too bummed out to go to school. And I figured that cutting school would get me into less trouble than going there and getting blamed for something else.

So I grabbed my coat, kissed my mom on the cheek, tried to ignore my old man, and ran out the door. I jogged three blocks in the bitter cold, watching my breath make little clouds in the air, and got to the bus stop just in time to inhale the diesel exhaust of the Number 22 bus as it pulled away. Figures. That left me with no choice but to get to the harbour on the good old foot-ankle express, as my mother calls it.

But guess what? I get to the old Angus MacDonald Bridge and they have the walkway blocked off because part of it is torn up. A big sign says "NO PEDESTRIANS" and there is a chain across the sidewalk. It's rush hour and the traffic is heavy in both directions. I'm pretty fed up by now with the fact that nothing seems to go right for me, so I say to myself, I don't care, I'm going to walk across the bridge anyway. A toll collector gives me a dirty look as I walk past him but I give him a fake smile and pretend I'm doing nothing wrong. And as I'm making my way across, trying to keep over by the curb, some jerk starts blowing his horn at me. Then another turkey slows his car, rolls down his window and says, "Get out of the traffic, kid. You don't belong out here."

Don't belong, that's a good one. And it's true. I don't belong anywhere. Thanks for the news. Like I really wanted his opinion. "Get lost," I tell him and smack a fist into the fender of his car with a loud *whump*. After that, I decide that if people can't give me a little room to just walk across this bridge, then why should I give them any? So I start walking toward Halifax right down the middle of the bridge, on the yellow line.

More drivers are blowing their horns. "Go ahead. I don't care!" I yell at them, realizing all these poor sad slobs are on their way to work like a bunch of zombies. They're trying to get there on time, just like my old man, always trying to play it by somebody else's rules. Not like me. I don't belong anywhere. I'm almost dizzy with the way I feel right now, finally standing up against the whole lousy world. I really *am* breaking the rules for once. I'm not just getting blamed for somebody else's mistakes.

I have this impulse. I want to know exactly what time it is and what I'm supposed to be doing. I check my watch. It's exactly 8:30. Home room. Mrs. Albro is taking attendance and I'm not there. I wonder if Denise even notices that I'm absent. I wonder if she cares.

"You dumb jerk," Dean said to me. "You're supposed to let the girl fall in love with you. Guys don't go tripping all over themselves and moping up and down the halls. Besides, she don't care about you, man. It's Harris now. You're history."

History. Maybe I should be history. Just get across this stupid bridge and keep on going and be long gone. As I walk, I lunge one way and then another, scaring the drivers, making them brake and squeal their tires or swerve out of the way. Suddenly, I feel this great sense of power.

I look up. Overhead, all the cables and railings are glazed over in ice. The sun is out and sparkling off everything. Over the harbour, the sea ghosts are swirling up from the water.

I'm in the middle of the bridge now, out over the harbour, halfway between Dartmouth and Halifax. I try to look in the frosty windows at the faces of the drivers as they go by. How come they all look like they're angry at me? It's because I'm a kid and I'm not playing it by the rules, that's why. What's the big deal? *Go on, get to work. Just don't think about what a stuffy stupid life you live. I'm never gonna be one of you.*

And suddenly, through their icy windows, I realize that all those white faces are looking at me, thinking I'm just another punk — a juvenile delinquent, or some kid who's flipped. I give one real pig-faced guy the finger. He tries to roll down his window to say something to me but it's frozen up with ice. I look at the other faces … all of them white … and I see the disgust. Maybe they do know I'm different, that I'm not one of them. I wish my skin would show it. They don't care what happens to me.

I look back out to sea, away from the jammed up cars. There's McNab's Island and, further out, Devil's Island. Beyond that, nothing but the ocean. I'm not paying attention to where I'm walking and I guess I walk right out in front of some guy driving towards Dartmouth. He slams on his brakes and I fall face-down on the hood of his car. I'm a little surprised but not hurt.

And as I'm shaking my head trying to clear my thoughts, I guess the guy behind him wasn't looking … wham! I hear somebody else smack into the rear of his car. I'm jolted forward on to the pavement and get the wind knocked out of me. Everything happens so quick.

I'm not hurt but a little dazed. The guy whose hood I fell on is out of his car now arguing with the driver who ran into him. A couple of other men are getting out of their cars. They're yelling something at me.

I hear a siren over on the Dartmouth side but the traffic's blocked. He can't get through. The whole picture starts to gel in my mind. They're coming for me. I'm the one who started this. Man, do I feel scared. I want to be away from here real bad. I want to be sitting in Mrs. Albro's home room. I try to get up but my whole body is shaking. People are screaming at me. My bare hands feel stiff from the cold and my muscles ache from hitting the pavement. I'm looking around at the faces of the other drivers but nobody gets out to help me. Nobody seems to care or want to get involved.

Then, about ten cars ahead, I see this old black guy get out of a beat-up stationwagon. He's running toward me, slipping and stumbling. I see his breath puffing like a steam engine. What on earth is he trying to do? I look the other way to see where the cops are but the traffic is having a hard time parting to let them through. And just as I look back to see what the old black guy is up to, bam, he's right over top of me, grabbing me by the arms and yanking me up off the pavement. As he pulls me to my feet, I can hear his raspy breath and see this look on his face that says he's scared to death. I can't figure out what he's up to. As he starts to pull me towards his car all I can do is sort of stumble along. I can't quite breathe right because I got the wind knocked out of me when I was thrown down on the pavement. My lungs can't find enough oxygen and I can't focus right. I want to say something, but I can't talk. Then I hear the siren again. He hears it too. We look at each other and I can see panic in his face. I've got to get out of here, I know. My legs start to work harder and we're nearly to his car.

He's got traffic to Halifax completely blocked and drivers look angry, worried and confused. People are still shouting at us but I can't understand what they're saying. He lets go of my arm and I continue to follow him. Why exactly do I keep on running with him? Why don't I just get away from here on my own? I look back towards the Dartmouth side and see nothing but snarled traffic and chaos.

We get to the stationwagon. He opens the driver's side and gets in behind the wheel. He looks really shaken, really scared. I'm just staring at him through the rolled-up window. I don't know what to do. Then he cranks down the window. "Get in!" he yells. "Other side." I do just that.

He starts her up and spins the tires on the salt and ice, all the while looking in the rear-view mirror. Once off the bridge he turns left down a side street, then right, then up a dead-end somewhere near Agricola Street. When he turns off the car, I'm leaning against the right-hand door, crying for the first time in long, long while.

"You better just sit here and cry, boy," he says to me, "because you sure got something to cry about."

Chapter Three

Larry

The old guy got out of the car and walked towards a two-storey wood-shingled row house. I sat there in the car for a few minutes trying to pull myself together until I felt the cold start to get to me. I was considering just taking off and not having to face this weird old character again, but something told me to follow him.

I walked inside the hallway of the house. The door to the first-floor apartment was open so I walked in. There he was, sitting at the kitchen table. He turned when he heard me come in.

"Why did you bother to get involved?" I asked. "Why do you care?"

The man pulled out a pouch of tobacco and began to roll a cigarette. He lit it, took a drag and coughed a long, painful cough. His eyes squinted down the way cigarette smokers do and he studied my face. "Because I seen you there, all scared and lost lookin', and I figured that I knew just what you were feelin' better than anybody else on the whole damn bridge."

"You could have got yourself in trouble, though. How come you didn't just drive off?"

"Well, I'm just stubborn, see. I was born stubborn. I'm not that smart, not that ambitious, but I tend to see a thing through once I get started. Besides, I could see that you are a bright young black man and I know that we need all the bright young black men available here in Nova Scotia."

Now I was a little freaked. "How'd you know I am black?" I asked suspiciously. Most people can't tell unless they know my folks or unless I say something to them. My skin is light and I have grey-blue eyes.

"Oh, I knew you were black alright, once I got a look at you. But it don't have that much to do with the colour of your skin. I got one look at you standing there in the middle of the bridge and I got a good look at your face and what I saw was the face of Darlington Sloan, the second best boxer that ever come out of Africville."

"Darlington Sloan was my grandfather," I told him. I hadn't heard anyone speak my grandfather's name in over two years.

"Then my guess was right. You are who I thought you were … Anne Sloan's boy."

"Corey," I said. "Corey Wheeler. My father's Carl Wheeler. Sloan was my mother's maiden name."

"Well it's good to run into you again, Corey Wheeler," he said, holding his hand out for me to shake. "Welcome to the home of Larry Sloan."

I looked hard at him wondering what his game was.

"Darlington was my brother," he said. "But he's dead now, as you know."

I knew all too well. "But then you're like an uncle or something to me." I finally grabbed his hand and gave it a shake as I let the news sink in.

"Or something."

"How come I never met you before?"

11

Larry punched out his cigarette. I watched the smoke swirl, thinking about the cigarettes that I didn't smoke that got me into trouble at school, thinking about how they had led me here to this strange old guy, my grandfather's own brother. "Oh, we met before, but you were only a little screaming kid in diapers then. I come over to see you and your mom quite a few times until your dad moved you out to the suburbs. After that, he let me know I wasn't exactly welcome."

Larry walked over to the wall and took down a framed black-and-white picture. He handed it to me. I recognized my grandfather. I recognized a younger version of Larry. "Who's the little girl with you?"

"That's Annie, your mom, and we're standing there in front of that house in Africville where Darlington and your grandmother raised her."

My head was buzzing and swimming around in circles again.

"Sit down there, Corey, before you fall down," he said, pulling up a chair behind me.

"Yep. I knew all the old families from Africville before they split us up. We used to call your grandpop 'Darling' Sloan. He'd get all riled but we knew he could take it 'cause he was about the best boxer ever come out of Halifax … 'cept for George Dixon, maybe."

"You a boxer, too?" I asked.

"Naw, I was never much of a fighter. People punch me, I just tend to lean back and let the punches slide off. I stay out of folks' way. Maybe that's why I outlived your old granddaddy. But people in the black community respect me for who I am and I'm very proud of that. I worked hard all my life and I'm always there for anybody who needs help."

12

Larry immediately noticed the sadness that settled back in on me like a dark winter cloud. I was thinking about my grandfather that I had hardly ever known.

"Corey, I'll fix you some pancakes. That's one thing I do right well. I make just about the best pancakes anywhere in the country. After about ten or twelve of my pancakes a man stops feeling sorry for himself. What do you say?"

I didn't say anything. I think I was too stunned by it all to answer. But I suddenly realized I was immensely hungry. I couldn't wait to see what Larry's pancakes would taste like.

Chapter Four

The Biggest Problem in the World

Larry explained to me about his job stocking the vending machines at laundromats and factory lunchrooms. "I fill the machines that sell pens and detergents and combs, that sort of thing. I got me one good coffee machine that makes good money. If I had any capital I'd buy a couple more of them."

I was gobbling up the pancakes and I didn't know what to say. It sounded like the dumbest, most boring job in the world. "You make a lot of money?" I asked.

Larry made a sweep with his spatula around the kitchen. "Maybe you ain't had your eyes checked in a long while. Look around. Do I look filthy rich?"

"Guess not," I said and stared down into the thick, gooey syrup on my stack of pancakes. "No offense, but you seem pretty old to me. Shouldn't you be like retired or something?"

Larry laughed. "You think everybody can just retire and go live in Florida? I got a pension comin' in but it's not enough to live on. So I gotta work if I wanna live. But I make my own hours and I'm my own boss," he said with a great sense of pride.

"I can dig it," I said. "You married?"

Larry poured the last of the batter into the black cast-iron frying pan. "Was married," he said. "Forty years. Then the good Lord came and took her away." It was the wrong question. I watched as the muscles in Larry's cheeks grew tight.

"Sorry."

He picked up the handle of the frying pan which must have been blistering hot. He walked towards me, holding it in front of him like it was a weapon.

When he was only halfway to the table, he gave the pan a flick and the pancake launched across the kitchen and landed squarely in the middle of my plate. He set the pan back down on the burner and rubbed the palm of his hand. "Sorry doesn't have a thing to do with it, son. Gone is gone. And that's all you can do."

"Right," I said. But I wasn't thinking of Larry's wife. I was thinking of Denise right then. Gone. History.

"What are you gonna do now, Corey?" Larry asked me, running cold water over his hand.

"I don't know."

Larry shook his head. "That's what all young people ever say. Makes me wonder how the country's gonna run when you grow up. It seems to me that I don't know is the biggest problem we got in the world … next to all them other big problems in the world, that is."

There was a knock at the door. Larry went to answer it.

"Hey, pops, how she going?" It was a black kid, a skinny dude in tough-looking clothes. He had razor cut hair like I'd never seen before except in the rock videos.

"She ain't going nowhere. We're just here eating breakfast," he said. "What are you up to, Darrell?"

"Nothing much, you know."

"As always. Well, *nothing much, you know*, I want you to meet *I don't know*."

Darrell walked into the kitchen in a kind of bouncy jive way like he was either about to break into a dance or maybe just playing it light on his feet in case somebody was about to take a poke at him. He eyed me with suspicion.

"Hi," I said.

"Yep," he answered, cool as frozen meat.

"Darrell," Larry said, "this here is Corey Wheeler. I picked him up ... hitchhiking on the bridge this morning. He looked hungry, so I offered him breakfast."

Darrell said nothing, just sort of bounced a little bit like he was bopping up and down to some bit of music playing in his head only he didn't have headphones on or anything.

"Turns out that Corey's my long-lost relative. This boy's the grandson of my brother. You remember ... Darling Sloan."

"The old boxer dude who's dead?"

"Right. I told you about him once."

"Yeah, but I don't get it," Darrell said.

I understood what Darrell didn't get. He had problems with the way I looked. I was getting real nervous as he came up way too close and studied my face. Something told me this mean little guy was about to pull out a knife and maybe lay waste to me right then and there. He seemed like a powder keg about to go off.

"You got a problem with something?" I asked, standing up and knocking my chair over backwards onto the kitchen floor.

"I don't think I'm the one with the problem," Darrell said. "I just didn't know they had come up with a pill to change your colour like that. That pill must have worked real good on you."

I had been razzed like this before. It was nothing new. White kids dump on me because I'm part black and black kids dump on me because I don't look black enough. Catch 22.

"Thanks for the pancakes," I told Larry and started for the door.

Larry was blocking it. "You ain't going nowhere like that, son. I helped you out. Now I feel like I got this sort of investment in you. Where you going?"

"I don't know."

"There, you're doing it again. Darrell, dammit, get over here and apologize."

"For what?" Darrell snapped.

"For nothing, that's what," Larry insisted. It was like they were speaking in code.

Darrell didn't say a thing but he cocked his head sideways and looked like he was trying to look hurt.

"That's better," Larry said. "What'd you come over here for anyway, Darrell?"

Darrell stiffened slightly again. "I came over to borrow five dollars so I can buy my mother some groceries."

"That's a lie and you know it. What about all those other five dollars I loaned you?" But already Larry was opening his wallet and pulling out a five-dollar bill.

"Forget about your mother," Larry said. "Take this boy down to the corner and buy him and you a couple cans of Pepsi. All I got is tea and he says he don't like no tea to wash down his breakfast."

"Sure," Darrell said. "C'mon."

I didn't quite know what else to do but follow Darrell out the door.

"You two stay away from the bridge," Larry called after us. "And Corey, you come back to visit again. But take a bus or something, boy. Don't go walking across that bridge alone no more."

Chapter Five

Blood Red

I followed Darrell up the street. He was walking pretty fast and I couldn't see what the hurry was.

"Where are we going?" I asked.

"You'll see."

We walked to the corner of Gottingen and right out into the street. Cars started honking at us and Darrell didn't even look to see if the drivers were stopping or anything. He just kept on going. Maybe I should have just forgotten about him and gone on home but this was the first time I was ever on my own in north end Halifax. Everything seemed so different that I wanted to check it all out.

I thought that Darrell was leading me to a corner store or something to buy the Pepsis but instead he took me into a hardware store.

"What are we doin' here?" I asked.

"Hey, man, relax. You're just along for the ride because you're a friend of Larry's. I got business and if you wanna come along, great. If not, kiss off."

We were walking up and down the aisles of this old hardware store looking at wrenches and hammers and power tools. Then Darrell stopped by some spray cans of paint. He started scanning the lids.

"Blood red," he said, reading the label. "That sounds good." He picked up the can and walked up to the cashier. I was still just tagging behind.

The man at the cash register was one of these real uptight-looking white people with a pinched face and a serious case of bad attitude. He gave Darrell and me a real dirty look that spelled trouble in my book but Darrell just handed over the five and took back a couple of dimes in change.

"Would you like a bag for that?" the man asked, real sarcastic like.

"Yes, sir, I believe I would," Darrell answered in a very formal way. "Thank you," he said. "Good day, sir." But as we were leaving the store, Darrell put the heel of his hand up to his face and made this loud fake farting noise that freaked out everyone in the store.

"It's okay folks," he said, "I was just practising."

Darrell was out the door and headed north on Gottingen. I was getting tired of tagging along.

"That's not what Larry gave you the money for," I said.

"Well, it's not like we had a contract. I got priorities."

We were passing by some stoned-looking guys who were hanging out in front of the Derby Tavern. "Hey Rattle," one guy said, "wanna by some smoke or whatever?"

Darrell just flicked out an arm like he was going to slap hands but he and the other guy just stroked air and we cruised on by.

"You get high?" Darrell asked.

"No way," I said. Sure, I've had a few beers and smoked a little hash but I wasn't about to get into that scene today. I had enough trouble. "Maybe I'll just take off," I said. I saw the bus stop up ahead. I could just get on the bus and head back to Dartmouth. If I wanted to, I could be back in school before noon. I'd make up some lie about being late. If I was lucky, or if I was good at pleading my case, I might be able to avoid another lecture from Hartman.

Darrell shook the spray can so you could hear the little ball inside bang around. "Some people on this street are dumb enough to spray this stuff into a paper bag and then sniff it until they get a good buzz. Kills off enough brain cells so you can't remember your name. Do it enough times, you'll end up so zoned out that you got nothing in your skull but fog."

"Sounds pretty lame."

"You're talkin'."

We were just past the library now and near the housing project at Uniacke Square.

"I like all those beautiful bricks," Darrell told me. "You know, for my art work. Watch this."

There were dozens of people walking up and down the street when Darrell casually walked up to the wall of the apartment building, shook the can and began to spray. He made big sweeping strokes but I couldn't make out what he was writing. I just stood back, pretending I wasn't with him.

Others had already written stuff on the wall. The biggest, boldest message said, "REMEMBER AFRICVILLE!" That was the second time today that name stung me.

Darrell finished. "What do you think?"

I couldn't make any sense of it. "What's it say?"

"What's the matter, they don't teach you how to read in school? It says, 'Rattletrap, Reeds and Tin Man.' "

Darrell looked at it and beamed like he had just created some masterpiece.

"What's it mean?"

"It's promotion, my man. I'm Rattletrap. Reeds and Tin Man are my professional associates. We're setting up a little DJ service with a little rap music and dance thrown in on the side."

Just then a big woman with a broom opened up the door of the building and came out swinging. She got a good one in on Darrell's head before he saw it coming and it sent him flying down on the sidewalk. His paint can went rolling off and, as he scrambled to his feet, he did a crab walk sideways to get it out of the gutter before starting to run.

The big woman was yelling, "You little low-life scum! I'll show you to go messin' up my walls." And I thought she was ready to chase Darrell on down the street but instead she turned on me.

I guess my reflexes were good, because I ducked just in time to miss the first blow and then took off like a bolt of lightning to get out of there. When I caught up with Darrell, we were both breathing hard. He punched me on the shoulder. "Man, that woman packed a wallop. Somebody should have that broom designated as a deadly weapon. She like to knock my head right off my shoulders."

I couldn't help but laugh. This started Darrell giggling.

"But why'd you go and do that to her wall?" I asked. "I mean, won't somebody have to clean it off?"

Now Darrell turned quite serious. "Ain't nobody going to clean it off. Besides, it's not her wall. The white people in the city built those little boxes for the black people to live in and keep them all in one place. They don't care about us."

I guess I looked confused because Darrell suddenly changed his tone. "But what would you know about that? You've crossed over the line. You keep your mouth shut and you can probably get away with being a regular white man for the rest of your life. Now wouldn't it be something to have a chance at that?"

Darrell picked up his can and started to walk away. "I got more public relations work to do. I think I better operate on my own, if you don't mind. Check in again when you're in town."

"Sure," I said. I watched him go, walking that bouncy jive down the concrete sidewalk like he was the king of something. We had run up Gottingen all the way to North Street and now I found myself looking at the cars driving out onto the bridge.

Something went funny in my stomach with all those heavy pancakes sitting there and all that running I had just done. I was just going to wait for the nausea to go away but I heard a car stop behind me. I turned around and saw that it was the bridge police. I didn't give the man a chance to get out of his car. I took off running back down Gottingen. When the coast was clear I'd catch the bus back to Dartmouth. I figured that I had had enough excitement for one day.

Chapter Six

Heartless Keeps the Lid on

Maybe I should have just gone to Penhorn Mall and hung out for the afternoon, but for some reason I really wanted to get back in school. I still felt pretty sorry for myself but after the events of the morning, what I wanted was a little less weird and a little more normal.

When I got to Thompson, the bell was about to ring for the end of lunch. Kids were still hanging out all around the school yard. I saw Harris and Dean but hoped they didn't see me. Too late.

"Coreycracker, where you been man?" Harris called out.

I walked over to where they were leaning against the wall.

"Look, I'm sorry about the Denise thing," Harris said. "I had no idea what the girl was thinking. All I did was ask her to go see a movie with me on Saturday. I mean, I knew she was going out with you but like I didn't mean it to be a big deal."

"It's okay," I said. I just wanted him to shut up. I didn't want to think about it. And I didn't want to have to explain it to Dean or anyone else.

"Well, it must have been my irresistible charm that overwhelmed the lady," Harris went on. "Still, I don't see why she had to dump you altogether. Fill us in on the deep background info."

I looked at Harris who had that confident smile on his soulful authentically black face.

"No, Harris," I told him. "It was just you, man. You just swept her off her feet. My loss. That's all."

But Dean wanted part of the action now. They both liked watching me squirm. "That's not what I heard," he said. "I heard it was because she didn't think you were black enough for her."

"That's just stupid," I said and I walked away. But it was out in the open now. Why did I bother hanging out with those turkeys anyway?

Dean ran on ahead when the bell rang. He had Phys Ed and that was something Dean was good at. Harris caught up with me as we made it to the door and walked inside the school. "You should've seen what happened in Harlow's class, Core," he said, all excited now.

"What?"

"Big John Barker is walking down the aisle when Dean sticks his foot out and trips Big J who falls smack on top of Cynthia Whitley. Then Dean says, 'The man must have forgot to tie his shoelaces. Get up off that girl, Johnnie.' Just then Harlow walks in and says, 'What's going on in here, people?' You know the way he always does. Dean just shrugs. John looks like he's ready to lose his cool. Instead, he says to Harlow, 'Just a little accident, Teach,' but as he turns around, he looks at the kids in the class and says under his breath but loud enough for most of us to hear, 'Just one of the niggers getting in the way is all.'

"Harlow didn't catch on but we all got the picture. Dean was ready to stand up and whack big John on the back of his head but I grabbed hold of his collar and sat him down. I was angry too, man, real angry, but I didn't want to see things go completely crazy. Besides, if they were sent to see Heartless Hartman, you know who would have been squeezed."

"Thanks for the blow by blow recap, Harris. Too bad I missed it."

"Where were you, Coreycrack, anyway?"

"Nowhere, man. Nowhere," I said. "Gotta go."

I turned to get away from Harris. I had about one minute to get to French class but I wasn't three steps down the hall when the principal's door opened, and there was Heartless dead stone cold in my path.

"Mr. Wheeler, there you are." The man had a face like a turnip and eyes like polished grey steel. He had streak marks up and down his neck all the time where you could see the razor tried to cut up his skin when he shaved every morning. Who could blame it?

"Sorry sir, I gotta run. I'm late."

"Late, Mr. Wheeler? I didn't know late was something that bothered you. Would you mind stepping into my office?"

Those steel grey eyes must have had laser vision too. I don't see how he had tracked me down that quick. "No sir, I wouldn't mind that at all. In fact, I had been thinking about stopping by for a chat some time." When in doubt, I tend to play things cute and sarcastic. Whatever trouble I'm in, it almost always seems to help double it but somehow I can't stop myself.

It was the old office scene. I knew this place like I knew my own locker. Heartless began to uncurl a giant paper clip. I sat perfectly upright like I was a straight A student about to be congratulated for outstanding performance.

"Corey," he began. He always went for first names once he had you seated in his office. He would pretend to be on your side, pretend to be friendly, then nail you to the cross. "Corey, I wonder if you could tell me what happened there in Mr. Harlow's class this morning?"

I immediately flashed on Harris' tale of blunder and hostility. But I was clean; I hadn't seen a thing. Too late I realized that I had already opened my mouth and said, "I don't know sir. I wasn't there this morning." *Idiot! Fool! Numbskull!* I shouted to myself as soon as I realized the words were out of my mouth.

Hartman smiled the smile of a Saturday afternoon TV wrestler who had just bounced the Cuban Crusader off the mat and is ready for the body slam. "I'm sorry. Did you say you weren't in class?"

Time to stutter. "Yes sir, that's right, you see …." But I had nowhere to go. My mind went racing down one side street of lies, and then another but I kept bumping into nothing but dead end walls. What was I going to tell him? I wasn't involved in anything in Harlow's class because I was hanging out with a graffiti artist in Halifax?

"What exactly should I see, Mr. Wheeler?" Formality now. "I had a good reason but I can't explain it. I was cutting class. You're right."

"Thank you." The confession pried out of me, Heartless seemed to relax. Now would come the long lecture. It would be death by boredom. "You know, Mr. Wheeler, if I were not such a tolerant man, I would simply throw your butt out of this school and you'd never come back. But I'm a fair man. I always treat my students fairly, no matter who they are."

There was something about the way he said that last part ... no matter who they are. What was that supposed to mean?

"However, now I'm also concerned about some growing tensions in the school. I have to look at the big picture and see where you fit into it. I'm beginning to get reports from the teachers about ... talk ... between students ... hostilities developing. It happens in any school, I suppose, but my job is to keep a lid on these hostilities. Do you follow me?"

"I do, sir." I had this absurd vision in my head of Heartless sitting his big fat behind on top of this enormous garbage can ... he was trying to keep a lid on it. Me and Harris and Dean and even John B and all his dumb friends were inside the can screaming and yelling, trying to get out. That was the way my imagination worked. I had this picture in my mind which was pretty funny and I guess I just sort of cracked a smile.

"Do you see something funny in this, Mr. Wheeler?"

Shoot. Why did I always have to take a bad situation and make it worse?

"No, not at all," I said. "I can see what you're getting at."

He wasn't convinced. "I'm afraid you don't realize that I will not tolerate fighting in this school or any provocations that lead to fighting. I don't care if the person is white or black or ... whatever."

Or something in between. Maybe that was what he was about to say.

Just then the buzzer on his phone rang. He answered it. "Yes? Right. I'll be there immediately." He slammed down the phone and got up out of his seat.

"See what I mean?" he said, pointing a finger at me. "Barker and that friend of yours, Dean, are trying to tear each other apart in the gym. I have to get down there. You get back to class and keep yourself out of trouble. I have this feeling that you might not be the one in the middle of the action all the time but somehow I have this hunch that you help make things happen."

I didn't feel like walking in late to French class. Even if I told the teacher I had been with the principal, everyone would look at me. I didn't want any more attention. I didn't want any more hassles. So I went and hid out in the lavatory until the bell rang for the next period. I sat in on my two final classes of the day but before school was over I had the opportunity to cop a zero on a math quiz and pull a D on a Canadian history test.

Later, I learned that Jenks had set up John Barker with Dean in a wrestling match during Phys Ed. Surprise, surprise. Barker slammed Dean down on the mat, pinned him hard, then pushed his face down into the mat. He held him there and wouldn't get off. Coach Jenks couldn't get Barker off until the principal showed up. And with my luck, I figured that Heartless would blame it all on me even though I was nowhere near it all.

Chapter Seven

The Mirror Must Be Lying

My mom sensed that there was something wrong as soon as I stepped in the door. She was sitting at the kitchen table reading that big fat textbook she studied for the night class at the university. She tried to hide the book when my old man was around. He didn't approve of her taking the course but she was too stubborn to let him stop her.

"You look like you had a rough day," she said.

"Yeah, I'm tired of getting blamed for stuff that's not my fault."

"Like what?" my mom asked.

I didn't feel like answering. I just shook my head and said, "You know, stuff." I went up to my room and put on my stereo full blast. It wasn't quite enough to blast the demons out of my skull, but I needed it. Then I remembered that my mom was trying to study downstairs. She'd never come up herself and ask me to turn it down. Not like my old man would. But why should I make life hard for her? Let her read her book, I figured. So I plugged in my headphones and cranked the volume up even higher. That was just right: heavy, loud music driving like a freight train in two ears at once until it crashed in the middle of my brain and drove out everything else. I sat like that for a full half-hour with my eyes closed.

When the tape was over and I opened my eyes, there was my mom, standing in the doorway looking at me. I swear she is the best looking older woman anywhere around. I like her dark eyes, her milk-and-coffee brown skin. I had to look away real quick because it was just too weird … too weird because I realized that she looked an awful lot like Denise, only older. I popped the cassette out of my tape player. Everything Larry had told me suddenly flooded back into my head. I wanted to connect all the loose ends about my family. I wanted to know exactly who I was and where I'd come from.

"Why'd you marry Dad?" I asked. It's funny I never came out and asked that question before because there was very little to like about my father. The man was angry about everything and he seemed to get angrier if anyone happened to be happy around him.

"I married him because I loved him," she said. A predictable answer.

"Yeah, but I mean, how come you didn't marry a black man? Did you hate being called coloured?"

Mom looked puzzled by my question but not shocked. "No, it wasn't like that. I think your father was just there at the time I was ready to settle down. Maybe I made a mistake, I don't know. But it was just a time when I had to get out of my mother's house. I had black boyfriends before, and a couple of white guys, too. But when the time came for me to claim my freedom from the rule of your grandmother, there was your father and he was offering to marry me."

31

"But what did you see in him?" It was hard for me to figure how this woman, my mom, who must have been a knock-out back then, could go for a man who yells if his dinner's not hot enough or if the slightest thing goes wrong.

"He's different now. He works too hard. He worries too much. It wasn't always that way. Maybe he'll change again."

"How come he hates it when we go to visit grand-mom in Preston? Why doesn't he come?"

"It's a long story, I guess, but back when your grand-father was alive, the two of them had a falling out."

"Darling Sloan," I said out loud, trying to remember that picture of my grandfather and my mother as a little girl.

"Yeah. How'd you know they called him that? We never called him that around here."

"Well, I ran into someone who knew him. Said he was a real good boxer … nearly the best." I wasn't sure just then I should reveal the exact source.

"Might be true, but it didn't do him much good. Once they pushed everybody out of Africville, his fists kept getting him into trouble. Including with Carl. When my father found out that I was about to marry a white man, he tracked down your father and gave him a good pounding. Carl and I never forgave him for that."

"He beat up Dad?" My father had always been a big muscular guy and I couldn't envision anyone giving him a thrashing.

"It was pretty bad. Your grandmother never said a thing about it. She pretended it didn't happen. And your grandfather was off on the circuit after that. But he was over-the-hill and should have quit. Got his head pounded one too many times and a blood vessel burst … but you know all that. It was that boxer from Montreal did it but nobody could say it was his fault."

I felt like I had learned more about my family in five minutes than I had in a lifetime. The pieces of my puzzling life were beginning to make a little more sense.

"But what was it you said about being pushed out of Africville? I don't understand."

My mother sat down on the bed beside me and looked across at the poster of Paula Abdul on my wall. "Not much to understand. Halifax had this big slum on their hands full of black people and they wanted it cleaned up. They also said they wanted the land to build a new bridge. And they wanted the all of us out. So pretty soon they were buying you out or just pushing you out and in rolls the bulldozers. I don't know how, but it seems to me somebody ended up making money on the deal and I tell you, it wasn't us. Your grandfather swore he'd fight back but it didn't seem there was anything he could do. They arrested him once when he tried to beat up a city alderman. With his fists, they called it assault with a deadly weapon. When he got out, he wasn't just a boxer any more, he was one mean punching machine."

"But that's not fair! How could they kick people out of their homes?"

She roughed up my hair and smiled. "Corey, who-ever told you life was fair? The truth was, a lot of those people didn't even own the land their houses stood on. Not in any legal way. They had simply been born there and their parents born there before that. I

33

was just a child then and, I'll tell you the truth, I was glad to get out of the city. Preston wasn't exactly like moving to Disneyland but we didn't have the city dump in our backyard, or the trains shaking the house in the middle of the night. The old folks didn't see it that way, though."

Downstairs the door opened. My old man was home. He slammed the door hard enough to make the whole house shake.

"I better go clean up my books," my mom said.

I sank back on my bed, my head reeling. That name "Africville" was stuck in my brain. And the image of my grandfather, who I had never really had a chance to get to know, was there too. I jumped up and looked at myself in the mirror. It wasn't right. What I saw there in the mirror was all wrong. I wanted that face to show my past. I wanted it to show who I really was. But there wasn't a thing I could do about it.

Chapter Eight

Bad News Laundromat

After school the next day, I caught the bus into Halifax and knocked on Larry's door.

"Who is it?" I heard a sleepy voice ask.

"It's me, Corey," I said. Then I heard him coughing hard and it sounded like he was having a hard time breathing.

The door opened. Larry had on old baggy pants, a torn T-shirt and suspenders. He had a couple of days' growth of white bristly hair on his face and he looked pretty rough. "Corey," he said with a smile. "It's a good thing you woke me up, son. I got to get on the road and service my machines."

"Can I come with you?" I asked. "I can sort of be your assistant." What I really wanted to do was talk, just talk, but I didn't mind helping out.

"Sure, sure. Come on."

Larry threw on an old ratty winter coat over his T-shirt and we walked down the stairs and out into the chilly afternoon. "You old enough to drive?" he asked.

"No. In a year," I said

"Too bad. I'd let you drive. I don't like driving myself. I don't like wrestling with all this traffic." I looked around and couldn't see even a single car coming down the street.

His stationwagon was maybe twelve years old. It was pretty beat-up with rusted-out doors. The front seats were shredded vinyl and the springs stuck through. Behind us, the back seat was down and the car was filled up to the roof with boxes. Larry cranked the engine over and it sounded like it had no intention of starting. "It's my chauffeur's day off," he said. "And if I didn't have people waiting for me, I'd just as well stay home and rest my bones."

He tried the ignition three times. The third try got her going and he pulled off down the street, driving at about five kilometres an hour. The man was the slowest driver I had ever seen and he checked his mirrors every two seconds to see if anyone was behind him.

When we came to the stop sign at Gottingen Street, I saw Darrell and two of his buddies on the corner. They had a big ghetto blaster about the size of my bedroom sitting on the sidewalk. It was turned way up and they were doing some crazy dance moves. People walking by didn't seem to pay any attention. Darrell had a microphone plugged into the blaster, and was talking rap over the music. I waved to him and he just dipped his sunglasses to acknowledge our presence. Part of his rap went like this: "If you want to party, you give us a call, for one low fee we'll do it all … that's Rattletrap, Reeds and Tin Man."

"What the hell is that?" Larry asked me, bending low to look out the window.

"I think Darrell calls it promotion."

"Well, he don't have to be so loud, does he?"

Larry turned right on Gottingen and we headed down to the south end of Halifax, stopping in front of the Blue Ribbon Laundromat on Henry Street.

Larry opened the back door with a loud groan of ungreased hinges and said, "You mind carrying that box?"

"No sweat."

The windows were all steamed up and the place was full of university students and mothers with little kids crawling all over the floor. I followed Larry to the vending machine and when he opened it, I could see that all of the slots were empty.

"Uh oh," Big Larry said. "Guess I underestimated. Crack open that box."

As I opened the big box full of little boxes of detergent, a heavy-set woman with a beet-red face came over to us. She had a mop in one hand and a mean disposition in the other.

"Where have you been?" she snarled with the voice of a wolf with a bad case of rabies.

"I guess I underestimated," Larry repeated to her.

"Underestimated? What kind of excuse is that? I got customers here cussing at me because you can't keep the damn machine filled!" she yelled, loud enough to attract the attention of every university student, mother and crawling rug rat in the place. Larry just looked straight down at the floor.

"I thought we had an understanding," she continued. "I don't need these customers yelling at me because you're too lazy to do your job and keep this machine filled on time. I'm telling you, this is the last time. If it happens again, I'll get somebody else to take care of these machines."

"Yes, I understand," Larry said, his head still bent over, his eyes on the floor. I was stunned. Why did he let her talk to him that way?

"And one more thing. I think you owe me and all these people here an apology," she said. What a stupid thing for her to do.

I was about ready to tell her to go clam up but Larry was already following her orders. "I'm sorry, ma'am. And I'm sorry if I've inconvenienced you folks."

I stood there silently as he bent over and filled up the slots inside the machine with the little boxes of laundry detergent. A few of the university students were laughing. I took a step toward the closest guy, ready to plant knuckles in his teeth, but Larry touched me on the shoulder. I stopped dead in my tracks, gave him a disgusted look and retreated to the car.

When he came back out and sat down, he rolled another one of his cigarettes. I could see his hand was shaking and he was breathing in short, raspy breaths.

"Why did you let her do that? And how come you let all those people laugh at you? You could have just told that old bag to shove her mop in her own mouth."

Larry wouldn't look at me. He started up the car. "Because, Corey, I need the money from this job to get by. It's what keeps me on my own, keeps me independent. You ever see what happens to other old people who don't have enough money to look after themselves? So I can't go telling off my customers. I can't."

"Well it stinks," I said. I didn't know who I was madder at, the laundromat witch or Larry. I sank low in the seat and folded my arms. I turned on the car radio but got nothing but static.

When we stopped at the Student Union Building at the university, Larry still looked pretty shaken up, like he was sick or something. "You all right?" I asked.

"You go in and do this one for me, okay? All you got to do is open her with the key and put those Bic pens inside, scoop out the money and lock her up."

"Right," I said.

It wasn't hard to find the machine but when I opened it up I saw that it was full. Full of pens, that is. There was change in the change-fill but nothing else. I guess none of the university students had bought a single pen. What a waste of time. I locked up the machine again and turned to go back outside but then reached down into my pocket. Six bucks was what I was carrying. I went over to the cafeteria cashier and asked for change in quarters.

In the car, I put the pile of change in Larry's hand and he seemed to have a hard time gripping onto it. The guy did not look good and his hand was down-right freezing.

"Man, you been to a doctor lately?" I asked.

He shook his head hard. "I don't like doctors. My wife never went to no doctor. She always cured herself. And then when she did finally go to see a doctor for the first time in her life, he sends her to the hospital where she don't last three days."

Larry didn't bother to pick up the quarters that had spilled out of his hand and onto the floor. I just sank down in the seat as he pulled away. It was a grey, dead-looking city, even here in the south end where the people with money lived. When we got back to the north end, it had begun to drizzle a freezing rain. Rattletrap, Reeds and Tin Man were gone. I guess they had given up on sidewalk promotion for the day. Larry parked his car over top of his favourite oil puddle on the street. He said he was going to go in for another nap, that he would be okay.

I caught the bus back to Dartmouth and my home in the suburbs thinking about what a dismal life Larry must lead. I started out feeling sorry for him, but by the time I got home again, I ended up feeling sorry for myself.

Chapter Nine

Shakespeare's Revenge

I guess I had started to turn old Larry into some sort of a hero in my head and it was pretty depressing to see that he was an out and out wimp. I wondered if this great respect he supposedly had in the black community really existed or if it was all in his head. But then I remembered how he had helped me on the bridge so I wasn't quite ready to write him off yet. Besides, he was my grandfather's brother. We were blood and that meant something to me, something important.

School was just a big pain in the butt. I tried to just stay clear of Harris and Dean so I didn't get sucked into any of the trouble brewing, but it wasn't easy. I didn't want to get in the middle of any battles they had going with Barker and his brood.

So there I was, sitting in Mr. Harlow's class getting good and bored over Shakespeare. We called Harlow 'the Deacon' because he always seemed so pure and righteous. Like every time somebody cursed in class, he'd get real upset. Most other teachers didn't care so much but the Deacon took it real personal and always looked kind of hurt about it.

So he's up there lecturing on and on about Hamlet somebody or other. I'm only half paying attention, which is about the most he'll ever get out of me, and I've begun this little list with the headings "Black" on one side and "White" on the other. My mom always says that when she can't decide between two things, she makes a list of the positive things for both sides. Sometimes, she says, she can figure out which side is better.

Well, I'm not having very good luck coming up with many good reasons at all as to why I want to be identified as black any more. I mean, even old Larry has turned out to be a disappointment and Denise doesn't want me. Even my grandparents couldn't stand up for their rights but allowed themselves to get kicked out of their own homes. I mean, what's the point? If I can already pass as white and if I just start acting that way, maybe after a couple of years people will just accept me as that and life will be a lot easier. So, on the positive side of being white I have no hassles, less grief, more friends ... which all sounds pretty lame, but on the black side, all I can come up with is better music, my mom, Denise (which I might just as well cross off) and for some reason I write down "AFRICVILLE."

Now that doesn't make a lot of sense because I don't hardly know anything about Africville and from what I do know, it sounds like it was a very big losing situation. But I've written it down in big dark capital letters. Well, I go back over to the white column and I write "better jobs, more money ..." but they just seem like empty words. I make one more entry in the black column — "Darling Sloan." Now that about covers it because I discover I'm not much good at making lists. I study the two columns side-by-side and realize that I'd be downright crazy to continue being black if I don't want to be. So I've half-decided I'm going to start making more white friends, find myself a new girlfriend who doesn't think of me as black and prepare for a new, happier and simpler life.

The Deacon is still droaning on and on about this Shakespeare play. It's all *tragedy* this and *tragedy* that and I think it's all a tragedy that it's so boring. So does Dean, apparently, because I look over and see he is sound asleep, his head bent over and a little dribble of drool leaking out of one corner of his mouth. I never saw anyone who could fall asleep in class like Dean. Well, the Deacon zeroes in on Dean catching the Zs and says, "Dean, why are you asleep in my class? God didn't give you a brain just so you could put it to sleep every day. Wake up." Even though the Deacon is probably pretty ticked-off, he keeps his cool and doesn't show it. The only problem is that Dean is so far off in wonderland that he isn't hearing Harlow at all.

That's when John Barker, elbows his football buddy Vic Swinnimer. Vic takes the cue and holds his open textbook up beside Dean's ear, then slams it shut, real loud, so that Dean jumps right up out of his seat he's so scared.

When he sits back down, he's shaking his head and saying, "Holy Moses! Where am I?"

And the class is in an uproar.

You'd think maybe the Deacon would say something to Vic but no, he just goes after Dean because he not only fell asleep through Mr. Shakespeare but woke up shouting blasphemies.

Harlow is still trying to keep it cool but the class is laughing and laughing and he has to raise his voice to be heard. "Dean, can you tell me the name of even one character in this play?" The Deac is holding his book high in the air now like it's a bird that wants to take off and fly right up into the sky.

Dean just sits there and looks embarrassed. The answer is pretty obvious. I lean over to whisper something but the lad is not fully comprehending the situation. I don't even think he knows what planet he's on. "Hamlet," I'm trying to tell him, but I can't get through the fog bank.

The Deacon is just shaking his head. He won't punish anybody; he's about to say what he always says at a time like this. Please pay attention. I'll forgive you this time but next time try to get it right. But those old familiar words haven't come out of his mouth yet. The class is settling back down and it's quieter and that's when John Barker says it. I think he only meant to say it loud enough for Vic to hear, but I hear it and so do the other kids. "Stupid nigger," John Barker says.

Dean looks like he is about to explode and the Deacon is shaking his head looking kind of hurt as if the insult was hurled at him. But me ... I don't even know what I'm doing, or why, but I've already closed my big six-pound textbook and I see my arm cocked back like I'm about to send a football on a fifty-yard pass downfield. Before I even have a chance to collect three brain cells and *think*, I let my English text fly. It whizzes past Dean and Vic and catches John Barker flat on the side of his head hard enough to knock him down onto the floor.

John's a bit stunned but then so am I because I don't hardly believe that I did the throwing. The last thing

I need in my life is another enemy and more trouble, but it looks like I just bought myself the round-trip ticket.

The poor Deacon is starting to pray, I think, because he's looking straight up at the fluorescent lights like heaven is right there, three feet above his head. Vic launches himself across Dean's desk straight at me, but Dean grabs him by the belt and tries to pin him down on the desk just like he's still in the gym and putting on a wrestling move.

Harris is on his feet now and trying to grab hold of Barker. And me, I'm still sitting there wondering what I've done. One of the other white guys has now grabbed Harris.

The girls are all yelling for us to cut it out, all except for Denise who is telling Harris, "Go on, Harris. Kick his white butt!"

Out of the corner of my eye, I see that the Deacon is on the intercom now and any minute I'm going to be in big trouble. Vic is still squirming on top of Dean's desk with Dean sitting right on top of him now. I see Vic's big angry pimpled face looking right at me and he has his teeth crunched together. He looks like a wild lion about to tear into supper. I don't like being near that mouthful of teeth so I stand up and begin backing my way up the aisle to the door. It could be that I'm not feeling too well. Maybe I threw the book because I was getting sick with the 'flu or something, and my mind wasn't working good. Yeah, that must be it, because it didn't feel like *me* doing it.

I'm at the front of the room now and Mr. Harlow is looking at me like he feels real bad about everything. I don't know what to say because the class is in chaos and it's my fault so I pretend like nothing's happened at all.

"Mr. Harlow," I say, "can I be excused?" But I'm already backing out the door. The only problem is somebody else is already trying to come through that same door and I bump right into him.

I turn around and there's Heartless Hartman, big and bad. He puts a stiff hand on each shoulder. I close my eyes and all I can do is shake my head and pray.

Chapter Ten

Stuck with Trouble

Well, once the whole story was out on the table, I was the only one who got suspended because I was the only one who did any real damage. That darn English textbook injured John Barker's ear so that he had to go to the doctor and get some sort of treatment. I did feel sort of bad about that but told Hartman that they shouldn't be giving us such heavy, dangerous text-books, that if I had had something lighter in my hand I wouldn't have hurt the sonofabitch.

"Don't use that language around me, young man," Heartless said.

"Language," I repeated. "That was what started it. Barker called Dean a nigger."

Heartless looked like he had just been visited by the ghost of his dead mother. "No one in this school is allowed to use racist language like that. No one."

And I thought that for once the man was on my side but he continued, "And in my entire ten years as principal of this school I have never heard one student use such a word. This is the 1990s, and people just don't talk like that any more. So you can just save your excuses."

Well, what was I supposed to do? Plenty of other people heard it and if I was to get them in here to back me up, Heartless would just say that I told them to lie.

"One week's suspension," the principal said, "and you better be glad I'm going so easy on you." The verdict was guilty and the punishment was no school. That didn't seem so bad.

My old man, though, went through the roof when I told him. "Why did you get involved? It wasn't your business. You could have just stayed out of it." He was fuming. It had been a rough day for him as usual. He had just polished off a beer and was now crushing the can in his hand and then twisting it around until it broke in half.

"I don't know what we're going to do with you. You've got to learn to just look out for number one. Forget about other people's problems. That's the only way you get by in this world. The guys I work with are always saying I should join this new union that's starting up, but I say a union is nothing but trouble and money out of your paycheck to boot. I stay in good with the foreman and I do my work. And that's what matters. When the lay-offs come, I hang on while other troublemakers go. There's a lot I gotta teach you, I guess."

I gave my old man a blank stare. I really did want to learn to like the guy but it was getting harder every day. It could be worse, I guess. He never hit me and he didn't really care how well I did in school as long as I graduated at the end of it.

My mom's reaction was different. She just cried and said it was all her fault.

"How can it be your fault?" I asked. But she didn't need to answer. I sort of understood what she meant even though it was stupid logic. I mean, if she wasn't my mother I would have never been born, right? And if she hadn't married my father, I wouldn't be the me that I am. Not that it was such a great deal being me.

So there I was, standing in the hallway, halfway between my father cracking open another can of Moosehead in the kitchen and my mother crying over her history book in her bedroom and right then and there I decided that I was stuck with being who I was. And apparently the me who had thrown the lousy textbook had decided he was black and, even though things looked pretty bleak when you took all the facts into account, I wasn't so bad off after all because I had a full week off from school.

Now I could sneak into Halifax in the days. I wanted to find out more about Africville from Larry. And I wanted to chase down Darrell, too, and see what he could teach me. I knew the dude was trouble, him and his paint cans, but I'd been trying to avoid trouble and look where it got me. I decided that if I was going to be bad and if I was going to be black, I might as well have some fun along the way.

Chapter Eleven

Rattletrap, Reeds and Tin Man

Suspension wasn't going to be that big of a deal. My parents both worked in the days. If they figured out I was splitting for Halifax each morning they'd kill me, but I couldn't just sit around watching game shows and *Sesame Street* on the tube.

I knocked on Larry's door. "Come on in. It ain't locked," he said.

I walked in. Larry was just sitting at the kitchen table drinking a cup of tea. He hadn't shaved in days. In front of him was a large scribbler like we used in school and I could see that it was filled with numbers.

"Aren't you supposed to be in school?" he asked.

"I have this week off. It's a special holiday."

"What's the occasion?"

"Somebody's birthday. I forget."

"You can't forget if that somebody is important enough to let children out of school for a whole week. He must be a pretty big deal."

I thought about it. Once you get yourself into a lie, it's important to be able to see it through.

"Michael Jackson. It's Michael Jackson's birthday."

Larry looked sceptical. "I thought Michael Jackson's birthday was next month," he said, "but I could be wrong."

Just then a woman upstairs began to sing. She had a big booming voice and was singing a song like something you'd hear in church.

"What are you doing?" I asked, pointing at the notebook.

But Larry had closed his eyes. "Shh, boy. Just listen. That's Irene. Listen."

I listened and all I heard was an old black woman belting out a song about dying and going to heaven. It sounded kind of sad and painful to me. But Larry still had his eyes closed and looked like he was floating off to heaven himself.

When she stopped, he said, "Now there's a woman who can sing. I'm glad that woman lives upstairs because I love to hear her do that."

"Sounds kind of unhappy to me. Why would you want to sit around and listen to an old woman sing about how bad she feels?"

Larry suddenly got very serious and gave me a look that could fry meat. "Corey, that singing is one of the few things that makes life worth livin' for me. I don't even hardly know that woman. I just see her in the hall and say hello. But when I hear her sing, I feel like my wife is still right here with me. And happy or sad, that song makes my bones feel like they are singin' too. Now that woman Irene, there's somebody they should have a holiday for. Not any old Michael Jackson."

"Sorry," I said. I could see that I had really offended him. "You going on your rounds today?"

"Yep, later. Wanna come?"

"Sure. What time?"

"Around eleven." Irene had started singing again and Larry started to close his eyes.

"I'll catch you around eleven," I said, getting up to go.

"Thanks. I'd like that," Larry said, fading off to glory and I closed the door lightly behind me. In the hallway I could hear the singing louder and clearer and it still sounded like some old corny thing to me. Funny what happens to an old guy. To think that a lonely woman's wailing song was about all that he had to live for.

I hoped that Darrell would be around somewhere not too far off. He had the life. No school at all since he'd dropped out. He seemed like a free man to me.

I finally found him hanging out with Reeds and Tin Man at the playground on Maitland Street. It was cold and blustery but these three guys just had on cut-down gloves without fingers and black leather jackets just barely long enough to cover their ribs. They were sitting on the swings like little kids but they looked like three mean customers. One of them had the blaster sitting on his lap but it was off.

"Hey dude," Darrell said when he saw me.

"Yo, what's happening?"

Reeds and Tin Man were giving me a hard look like I had just stepped out of a sewer of something.

I knew which one was Reeds because he had his name in big red letters written on the front of his jacket. Reeds took a look at me and said, "What is this, Rattle?"

Darrell smacked him. "This is my friend Corey. Corey lives out there in the suburbs. This is what happens to black people who move into the suburbs." Reeds and Tin Man just laughed. I shook my head. What could I say? It was kind of funny.

"No school today, Corey?"

"I got suspended."

"All right," Reeds said. I could see that his suspicion was fading to admiration.

"So what are you guys doing?"

"We're waiting for somebody to walk by and give us a million dollars. What's it look like we're doing?" Tin Man said.

"How's the promotion going?" I asked Corey.

"Not bad, not bad. We might have a gig working for Freddy Reacher. He's got a party coming up."

"Who's Freddy Reacher?"

The boys looked at me like I didn't know anything. I didn't.

"Freddy's pretty important in the community," Darrell said. "Myself, I don't approve of his trade but if he wants us to DJ and rap, we could use the work."

"You see a long white car with dark window glass all around, that's Freddy," Tin Man said. He pointed to a slogan sprayed on the handball backboard: "What Fred Said!"

"I don't get it," I told him.

"That's 'cause you don't live here, little bro."

"Time for a little more promotion work," Corey told me, pulling that same spray can of blood red out of his back pocket. Right below "What Fred Said," he sprayed "Rattletrap, Reeds and Tin Man" in that almost totally illegible style of his. He looked real pleased with his work. "Now you." He handed me the can.

Chapter Twelve

One Good Move

I couldn't think of anything to write. I tried to hand the can back. Spray painting on walls seemed too dumb to me anyway. But Darrell had his arms folded. The boys were looking awful disappointed.

"Okay." I gave the can a hard shake then sprayed, "Remember Africville," just like I'd seen on the wall at Uniacke Square. I handed Darrell back his can.

"All right," he congratulated me, and set the can down on a picnic table. Reeds popped a button on the blaster and a loud thumping rhythm started up. He set the blaster down on the frozen playground and began to talk in that angry, cool talk that rap singers do, all the while doing some kind of crazy martial arts routine. He punched out his fist and kicked up his foot as high as he could.

Tin Man and Corey joined in and did a kind of outer space dance while rapping through a song which must have been something they made up. It was all about dealing dirt on Gottingen Street and people getting knifed at the Derby Tavern and then somewhere toward the end they said, "But we still can't forget, and we ain't gonna let, them do it again — Africville."

The song ended on that word. I let out a howl 'cause it sounded so together. When I clapped and whistled, the guys looked like a man *had* driven up and given them a million dollars. And suddenly I felt good. I mean, I felt like I was part of something though I didn't quite know what.

"You didn't tell us what you got suspended for," Darrell said to me, suddenly interested in what I was all about.

I told them the whole story about Dean and about Barker.

"Sounds like you better be ready if those jocks decide to get back at you," Tin Man said. "They might not figure getting suspended from school is punishment enough."

"I can handle myself," I lied, trying to sound tough.

"You carry anything?" Tin Man asked.

I wasn't sure what he meant. I shrugged.

"You know. Knuckles? Knife? Anything?"

"No," I told him.

Suddenly Reeds, the biggest meanest looking one of the three came over real close and stared down at me like he was about to threaten me. "You sure you know what you need to know to protect your ass? You got any moves?"

Again I shrugged.

Reeds gave me a look of disgust. He turned sideways and like lightning, his leg kicked out and he sent the seat of the swing up over the top bar. As it came back down on the other side, I had to duck so it didn't smack me on my head.

"You can kill somebody with a move like that if you have to," Darrell explained.

"I don't think I want to kill anybody," I said, really wanting to drop the whole subject. I didn't want to think about my problems at school and I really didn't like thinking about Barker and some of his goons still trying to get even with me.

Reeds, however, didn't want to let it drop. "I been studying martial arts a long time, man. I don't intend to kill nobody either. However, it's always good to know you have the power even if you don't ever use it. You, for example, ain't that big. Sometimes you have to know what to do if somebody bigger than you wants to walk on your face."

I guess Reeds could tell that I wasn't convinced so he suddenly grabbed my arm, spun me around and yanked my arm up hard behind my back, pulling on it like a lever in such a way that I felt pain shooting all the way to to my neck.

We stood like that for a second, frozen stiff. I was afraid to move. I could hear Reeds breathing down my neck. What was it with this guy? I didn't do anything to hassle him.

"Easy man," Darrell said. "Corey's my friend. Don't break his freakin' arm." Tin Man, meanwhile, just stood off to the side with his arms folded like he knew what this was all about.

I sucked in oxygen and hoped that Darrell would figure out a way to get me out of this situation with all my bones intact. What was I supposed to say, anyway?

"The point is, little brother," Reeds said, applying and releasing pressure to prove to me that he had complete control and could cause pain with just the slightest pressure, "the point is, you don't need to know all about kick boxing or Kung Fu or Ju Jitsu to save your own butt. Sometimes you only need to know one good move. Like this one.

"You learn this and you know how to break your opponent's arm if you have to. You only use it if and when. Maybe once in your life. After that, whoever will stop messin' with you. All it takes is a little practice." Reeds let go and gave me a gentle push.

I wasn't sure whether to laugh or cry. I decided it couldn't hurt to learn. I was afraid to say no. Besides, whoever said that the only education you get is inside the four walls of a school.

So Reeds taught me how to put any poor slob into the lever-arm lock. He showed me how size and weight didn't matter. You could use your opponent's strength to work against him. I practised on Darrell, then on Tin Man and finally on Reeds himself. Each time I got them fully into the position it was clear that I could break each of their arms if I wanted to. The new sense of power I now felt wasn't so much from learning the move, it was from the kind of trust I felt in these guys.

"Just keep practising, Corey," Reeds said. "Practise in your head if nothing else, until it becomes like instinct."

"Thanks," I said.

Just then a Halifax police cruiser turned the corner and Darrell looked kind of nervous. I saw the paint can sitting on the picnic table in front of us. I grabbed it and stashed it under my jacket.

"What are you so uptight about, Corey?" Darrell asked. "You ain't got nothing to get busted for."

"Nothing but a paint can," I said.

"Sit down. We can't go jumping up every time somebody looks at us the wrong way," Tin Man said.

So I picked an empty swing and sat down alongside the brothers there in the cold wind. The cops did stop and just sort of gave us the once-over but they never got out of the car. I saw the driver pointing to the handball backboard where I had sprayed my message but that was it. Then they just drove off and let us be.

Chapter Thirteen

Africville Ghost Town

After hanging out with Darrell and his buddies, I was feeling pretty good about myself but as soon as I sat down in Larry's old stationwagon and we began heading off, I started to feel bad again.

Larry would drive so slowly in that old battered car that people on the sidewalks stared at us. They figured we were a real hard-luck case. And I guess we were. I was a refugee from Dartmouth, suspended from school, and here I was hanging out with this frail old dude who had a nickel-and-dime operation stocking vending machines around the city.

"How old are you anyway?" I asked Larry. I was just trying to start up a conversation. There was too much dead air in the car.

"I'll be seventy-two come April."

"That's old."

"You're right. Real old. Stay young, son. Don't ever let yourself get old."

"I'll try to do just that," I said. I could never picture myself being as old as Larry. If things got that sorry, I think I'd just hang up my skates. "Why don't you, like, retire or something?"

"Retire to what? I told you, the pension wouldn't be enough to live on and I don't want to be no welfare bum or be put in some government home. I only have a few dollars in the bank. So I just have to keep on doing my job."

I wanted to say that it wasn't much of a job. All he did was fill vending machines with soap and pens and geeky toys for fifty cents. But I kept my mouth shut.

The first stop was the Acadia Lines bus station on Almon Street. A few people were snoozing on the vinyl chairs. It wasn't a busy time. I carried the supply box and followed Larry into the men's room where he opened a dispenser of combs, toothbrushes and other odds and ends. He collected the money which couldn't have amounted to more than three or four dollars. Guys walking in gave us a sort of disgusted look, like we were there to rip off the machines or something. It made me feel real paranoid and I didn't exactly like the idea of hanging out in public washrooms, anyway.

When we went back out into the lobby, Larry said, "You see how it's done? Think you could do it by yourself if you had to?"

"Yeah," I said. "No big deal. I could do it."

But I didn't realize it was a trap. "That's good, son. You're a fast learner. Go check on that one inside there. I'll wait out here."

Larry pointed to the door of the ladies' room. "No way, José."

"It's all part of the job. I thought you said you could handle it."

"Yeah, well ..."

"Well, look here." Larry walked up and knocked at the door like he was visiting an old girlfriend. "Hello?" he said. "Anybody home in there?" There was no answer. The few sleepy bus passengers were giving us funny looks.

"There, you see. Nobody home. The coast is clear. Go on in."

Well, I couldn't just chicken out. I'd never been in a women's washroom before and I wasn't positive that the place was empty. I mean, who inside there would say, "Yes, I'm home. What can I do for you?" But I walked in anyway with the refill box.

Wouldn't you know it. There was a woman in there. She was staring at herself in the mirror and putting on make-up. When I walked in, I thought she was going to blow a gasket.

"Pardon me, ma'am. I just came to check the vending machine," I said, setting my box down on the floor. I had surprised her I guess and she had accidentally smeared a big red gob of lipstick across her face so she looked like she was getting ready for a circus. I wanted to laugh but I held it in. Then she grabbed her purse and began to tromp out of there. She didn't say a word.

Well, I went ahead and refilled the machine and put the money in my pocket. When I walked back out, there was old Larry with a big ear-to-ear grin on his face. "Did she do any damage to you?" he asked. And I looked at the others in the bus lobby. They were laughing. Laughing at me.

I didn't say a thing as we walked out of there. When Larry sat down at the wheel of his car, he slapped his thigh and shook his head and laughed out loud. "You should have seen the face on that woman when she come out of that washroom," he said. But I knew the joke was on me, not her. It wasn't until we were at the third stoplight that Larry asked me, "By the way, was there any money in the machine?"

I had forgotten all about it in the humiliation. I shoved my hand in my pocket and dumped the money on the seat beside me. I felt embarrassed again. "I wasn't trying to keep it, you know. I just forgot."

"I know, son," Larry said. "I was just checking. Besides, I had so much fun back there that I think you should just keep the money."

But I wasn't about to touch it again.

We were all the way up to the top of Robie Street and on the approach to the other bridge, the one they still called the new bridge even though it was already twenty-some years old. Cars were honking their horns at us because we were going too slow.

"You know, you can get a ticket for driving like this. The cops could pull you over because you're obstructing traffic. If it happened enough times, you could lose your license."

I don't think Larry ever thought about that before. He had that little bit of fear in his eyes again. "Then I'd be in big trouble," Larry said. "I couldn't fill my machines." He tapped down on the accelerator a bit and we got moving at a sensible speed.

We were on the bridge now, a big four-lane deal that pulled us up into the sky over what they call the Narrows of Halifax Harbour.

"Look down there on the left, Corey. You were asking about it."

"About what?"

"Just look."

All I saw were loops of curved asphalt — the roadways leading up to the bridge and, beyond that, a park of some sort. The grass was all dead and there was trash blowing around there. Further back was a container pier with big monster ships three city blocks long. "I don't get it," I said.

"Africville. That's what it looks like now. See that little park there. Almost no one goes there because it's surrounded by all these highways. Then you got a few warehouses and stuff and that big container pier for ships. Ain't nothing left of where I grew up. Used to be all homes down there, but not any more."

Chapter Fourteen

Just the Way Things Are

I looked long and hard at what used to be Africville, twisting my neck back around as we drove across the bridge. The sunlight was strong and it sparkled off the water of Bedford Basin to the north.

"But things worked out the way they was supposed to," Larry said.

"The hell they did. It wasn't fair and it still isn't fair. White people dump on black people any time they get a chance. They want it all and they don't care who they kick around," I said. I was still feeling angry about that scene at the bus station and I wanted to be angry at someone. It was impossible to stay mad at Larry.

"I used to think it was that simple. I figured they were the bad guys and we were all nice people. But that's not always the case. Take for example, my one-time friend named Reginald. Reginald grew up living right near your grandfather and me there in Africville. When we got older, Reginald and me got into business together. Then one day when I turned my back, Reginald just about stole me blind. I found out then what I should have known all along: the colour of your skin don't say that much about what kind of person you really are."

I was thinking now of John Barker and his friend Vic, the bastards. I was thinking about the way that Hartman talked to me and the way that he treated my mother when she was in his office. "No, you're wrong, Larry. It does make a difference. Sometimes you just have to take sides. Africville isn't over yet."

Larry came to a stop at the toll booth and was trying to find fifty cents in the change I had tossed on the seat. A line of cars had pulled up behind us, but Larry didn't seem to pay them any attention.

He got real serious all of a sudden. "I think I'm beginning to see what your problem is, Corey. You don't know who you are. And you're starting to come to the wrong conclusions."

"What do you mean?"

"I mean that in the long run, we will all be dead and buried and it don't matter when your bones rot back into the earth what colour your skin has been."

A commissionaire was walking toward us to see if there was some trouble. Six cars were backed up behind us. Larry began to roll down the window. I had distracted him and he still hadn't picked up the fifty cents to throw in the basket. I pulled two quarters out my pants and heaved them past him straight into the basket. The light turned green but he still didn't give it the gas.

"What I'm trying to tell you is that you don't have to take sides. It ain't no war going on and if it ever comes to that, we are all as good as gone. Just forget about being one of us or one of them and be yourself, whoever you are. That's all that matters."

The commissionaire was at the window now, standing there looking like a military general. "Is there a problem here?" he asked.

"No, sir. A small difficulty. But we're fine now."

"Then move it, Pops. You're holding up traffic."

Larry put the car in gear and we drove off.

The conversation had ended. He changed the subject. "You're about to see my pride and joy."

"I can't wait," I said, feeling a little put off by the way he had been lecturing me.

Larry pulled up in front of a tool and die plant in the Burnside Industrial Park and he grabbed a new box of something. Inside, we walked past the receptionist. She just nodded a hello and we went to a small lunchroom with about a dozen vending machines.

"They're not all mine," Larry confessed. "But this one is."

He was stroking the side of a coffee vending machine like it was a brand new Trans Am or something.

"This is your pride and joy?" I asked.

Nobody else was in the room but he whispered to me anyway, "I make over ten dollars a week profit on this baby. Watch this."

He turned the key like he was starting up a sports car and the front of the machine popped open.

"Water hooks in there. It gets heated up, and then the instant coffee falls down into the cup from there and bingo. You can push for sugar or whitener or whatever. Here, have one on me."

Before I could tell him I didn't drink coffee, he made it whir into action. The paper cup fell down right into place and in a second I had steaming hot cup of black liquid.

He could tell I wasn't impressed and went about his work refilling the instant coffee and whitener, collecting the money, and refilling the change slot.

He serviced one other pen and comb type machine and we turned to go. Just then a short, heavy-set guy with a cap that said "Foreman" came into the room.

"Larry, I'm glad you're here," he said, his eyes directed more to the wall than to us.

"How are you, Mr. Arthur?"

"I'm just fine. Just fine. We're real busy here these days. You?"

"I'm okay...." I was sure Larry was about to say more, just small talk, conversation, but he was cut off.

"Look, I have to tell you that this machine has to go," Mr. Arthur said. He was pointing to Larry's pride and joy.

"Why? Isn't it working right?"

"No, not that. It's working fine. It's just that we've got a new contract with these other people here who are going to do all the food and drink machines. It's a big outfit from Toronto and they say they want to run all the machines or nothing. If we lose them, we lose the candy machines and the men will be pretty grumpy about that. So our hands are tied."

"But I thought we had an agreement."

"Nothing on paper that I can remember. Look, I'm sorry it has to be this way. But could you have it removed by next week?"

So this was Larry's life — heartbreak on top of heartbreak, even over something as stupid as a coffee vending machine. I wanted to see Larry stand up to the guy. He had nothing to lose. He could tell him off.

Instead, he said, "I'll be sure to have it out of here by next Thursday."

The man smiled. "Thanks. I'm busy. Gotta go." And he walked out the door.

Back in the car, I chewed Larry out. "You shouldn't let him push you around like that. What's wrong with you?"

But Larry just looked straight ahead out the windshield and said, "It's all right. No point in getting all riled up. That didn't mean nothing. That's just the way things are, that's all."

Chapter Fifteen

The Invisible Man

It was an interesting week, to say the least. I learned stuff I never would have picked up in school. I hung out with my friends … Darrell and Reeds and Tin Man and, of course, Larry.

On Friday, however, I came back from Halifax at around three-thirty and found my mom home early from work.

"Where were you?" she demanded, sounding pretty frantic.

I don't know. I just didn't feeling like lying so I told her I had met this old guy named Larry who I was helping. I explained about his job and that I was a sort of assistant.

She knew instantly who I was talking about. "You've been going to see my uncle?"

"Yeah. I really like the guy. We've become good friends." I decided this was enough news for one day. I wouldn't try to explain about my other friends — Rattle Trap Darrell, Reeds and Tin Man.

"How'd you meet Uncle Larry?"

Well, I fudged it a bit. I couldn't tell my mom about the bridge. I said that I met him in the parking lot of Penhorn Mall, that his car tires were slipping on some ice and he needed a push to get going. I said he offered me a part-time job helping him with the vending machines.

"Is he still living in the same place, that old first floor apartment in the north end?" she asked, still not comfortable with the whole idea.

"Yeah, I guess he is."

She seemed real flustered. It was partly because she thought I had been home every day all week, but I also think it was the connection I had made with someone in her family. I bet she was thinking about her own father. She never talked about him much and neither did my grandmother up in Preston. Now my mom seemed confused, kind of lost in her own thoughts.

"Well, don't tell your father. I don't think he'd understand."

"I won't."

"But you tell me the truth from now on, and if you are going into the city, you tell me first."

"Yes."

"And I'm going to talk to your grandmother to find out what Larry's been up to. I need to find out what sort of man he is these days."

"That's fine."

"Now, you and I are going to do some serious homework," she said. "Get out your books and I'll get mine."

"Sure thing." And the first thing my mom did was to get on the phone and call up some of my teachers to ask about my assignments. Then we both sat down and did homework for two hours straight until my old man got home. And for maybe the first time in my life, I really felt like doing the work. After supper, while my old man was planted in front of the TV watching "Three's Company" and "Who's the Boss?" reruns, my mom and I kept on working.

Monday morning at school was something else. Harris, my good buddy who had stolen Denise away from me, put his arm right around me and said, "Good to see you back, Corey." We were outside the school and the buses were pulling up, unloading wave after wave of Thompson High kids.

Dean and Harris showed up just then. "Man, you're some kind of hero," Dean said.

"Get real," I said, not taking him seriously. I saw Denise headed our way, too, and I really didn't want to see her because of what she had done to me.

I tried to look away but she grabbed my chin in her hands and said, "Maybe I was wrong about you," and gave me that big sweet, sassy smile that melted the buttons on my shirt.

Harris just shook his head. "Easy girl," he said to Denise and she gave him an elbow in the ribs.

"Just stay out of Hartman's way, Corey," Dean told me. "I'm not sure he's done with you. The heat is on."

"What are we talking about? I paid my dues. One week suspension. That's over. I'm good as gold."

"Over nothing," Denise said.

That's when she saw some of her girlfriends and took off to meet them. The bell rang and people were scrambling for classes. I ran too.

I rounded the corner in the hallway. There was Barker and Vic and a couple of other guys from the wrestling team. They were burning holes through me with their dirty looks but nobody said anything.

I was about ten feet past them when I stopped dead in my tracks. I *had* hit Barker in the head with one heavy book. And I wanted to say something to put it all behind me. I walked back. "John, I'm sorry man. I don't know what came over me."

Vic and a couple of the other goofs just laughed out loud. Barker said nothing but stood there, his chest all puffed up, and breathed heavy like he was trying to press a 200-pound barbell. Out of the corner of my eye I saw Heartless humming along through the thinning crowd. I wasn't about to hang around and keep this up. I split for home room where I just wanted to sit down, keep my mouth shut and pretend that everything was normal.

No matter how much I tried to ignore it, I could tell that other kids were looking at me. Some of the black guys were showing the fist and smiling like it was some sort of signal I should understand.

"Welcome back, Mr. Wheeler," Mrs. Albro greeted me as I walked in the room … like I really needed the extra attention. I buried my head in my math book, tried to ignore the signals from Dean and Harris.

What I couldn't ignore were the looks I was getting from the white kids. Some of them were studying me like I was a new student who had just arrived from the planet Neptune, but others, even girls like Tina and Melissa who I used to chum around with … they were giving me a hard, mean sneer like I had committed a major felony.

I guess I realized then that I had chosen my colour after all … or maybe they had chosen it for me. The trouble is that what I really wanted right then was to be invisible. I wished that no one could see me at all.

Chapter Sixteen

The Same Old Trap

I sat quiet as a brick wall through Math and English, and world problems where we discussed nuclear disarmament. Man, nuclear war seemed to me to be the last thing that I had to worry about right now. I kept thinking about Africville and the way I saw Larry get pushed around. Why the heck was he willing to take it? Why didn't he stand up for himself instead of saying, That's just the way things are? How come the black community wasn't fighting back?

And it began to sink in that I was a lot more like Larry than I wanted to admit. I had taken the rap for the fight in Harlow's class. I had stopped trying to convince Heartless that I was innocent of half the things he accused me of. It just seemed that I was always at the wrong place at the wrong time. While the other kids around me were discussing war and peace, I was thinking that maybe none of us should take it any more. Maybe I did the right thing when I threw the book at Barker. Maybe it was only the beginning. Maybe it was time to fight back.

The bell was about to ring for noon hour. I walked out into the hallway and was headed towards the cafeteria when I realized that I had forgotten to bring a lunch and I had no money in my pockets. I checked my watch. If I ran my legs off, I'd be able to get home and grab some food and be back in time for my next class. I was starving. Food was a necessity. I turned around and started towards the doors when this locker pops open in front of me and just about flattens my face. I stopped dead in my tracks.

It was Denise. "We're all real proud of you, Corey," she said.

"What? You're crazy, girl." I tried to brush her off. I just kept on walking. I think I had already developed an instinct telling me when a woman was going to bring me nothing but trouble and this was one of those times.

"Walk you outside?" she asked. She already had a hold of my arm.

"Not going to the cafeteria?"

"No, I thought I'd go outside if you were going out."

"Yeah, well I forgot my lunch," I said. "I'm gonna walk home and get something. See you."

Denise seemed puzzled at my brush-off but I didn't care. I was out the door and seeing nothing but sunlight in my face and ignoring everything I could ignore. To tell you the truth, I was kind of looking forward to just getting on the old foot-ankle express and running like the wind, but I wasn't two steps out the door when Dean latched on to me.

"I never did thank you," Dean said.

"It's okay, man. I didn't do anything for you. I did it for me."

I was walking at a pretty fast clip and couldn't seem to shake Dean. "Where you going?" he asked.

"Home," I explained again as I walked around the corner of the school building. I was going to take the short cut through the bus parking lot around back and across a couple of backyards. "I need to get some food, okay?"

"I'll come with you. I need the exercise," Dean said but there was something funny in the way he said it. I heard worry in his voice and I saw this paranoid look come over his face.

"What is it with everybody?" I asked. "I'd rather just be left alone sometimes." I don't know why I was being so negative to everybody. "Why do you wanna go tagging along with me, anyway?" We had just turned the corner at the back of the school.

Dean was looking past me at something. I could tell from the look on his face that it wasn't good news. "Well, Corey," he began, "I had this hunch that, like, maybe you shouldn't go off on your own … just in case somebody came looking for you.…" He cut off in mid-sentence.

"And?" I asked, afraid to turn around and get the whole picture.

"And I was right, dude."

I turned around. There, coming out from behind one of the parked buses, were Vic and Barker.

"They were counting on you being alone, Corey-crack. Aren't you glad I came along for support?" Dean was actually smiling like he was looking forward to this. I made a quick calculation of what we were up against and decided that the total weight of Vic and John was maybe 100 pounds more than little Dean and myself. But Dean was already smacking a fist into the palm of his other hand.

Time seemed to slow down just then and I had a chance to think before I said anything stupid. I realized, that despite all my daydreaming about fighting back, I knew that this wasn't the way I wanted to do it. This was the same old trap I'd always fallen into. Whatever happened here, it was gonna be the same old story for me — wrong time, wrong place. If we won or lost, I'd probably be kicked out of school for good and be poking around some empty playground in the winter with guys like Darrell, Reeds and Tin Man.

Chapter Seventeen

Seeing It Through

Vic and Barker were four feet away. There was nobody else in the back lot. I didn't want to have to go through with this. It wasn't that I was scared. In fact, I felt like I had already run through the dress-rehearsal. I had practised — in my mind at least — that one move that Reeds had taught me. I knew at this minute that if I wanted to, I could break the arm of either one of these jerks. Sure, they were both bigger but I could use their weight to my advantage, just as Reeds had said.

I looked John Barker right in the eyes and said, "I don't want to fight. We're just gonna walk on by."

"No you're not," Barker said. "You're not going anywhere until we get even." Barker and Vic had positioned themselves directly in our path.

I should have been worried but what I felt was tired. It seemed that all my life I'd seen kids fighting each other like this over one stupid thing or another. Barker and Vic, despite their size, reminded me of two little punk kids and I didn't want anything to do with them.

"C'mon Corey," Dean said, "let's show this scum who they're messin' with."

"Forget it," I told Dean and shook my head. I started to walk around Vic and Barker, but Dean stood his ground.

"At least one of you isn't chickenshit," Vic said and dove for Dean, tackling him around the waist and pushing him down to the asphalt. Barker got in a couple of solid punches right into Dean's face before Dean could roll over to one side and kick himself free from the big creep.

It was hard but I was holding back, I swear. Barker was just looking at me and smiling, waiting for me to make a wrong move.

Then, just as Dean had got himself back up to his feet, his nose dripping bright red blood, Barker turned from me and gave Dean a sucker punch right in the eye. Poor little Dean reeled backwards into the brick wall and then fell to the ground, this time with both goons pounding him.

That was it for me. No way could I just stand by and let Dean get wasted by two dumb jocks. I grabbed Barker from behind and heaved him off Dean. Barker came up swinging but I ducked and swerved. I gave him a shove that sent him sprawling, then I tried to pull Vic off without much luck. With me pulling and Dean jabbing at the guy's gut, he finally took a hint and started to stand up. Dean got quickly to his feet and butted his head into Vic's belly. It looked like he maybe knocked the wind out of him because Vic staggered backwards and tried to regain his balance. I grabbed for Vic's arm and began to bend it up against his back the way Reeds had taught me. Amazingly, it worked. I had him perfectly in control. If he tried to get away from me, he'd be in serious pain. And I could have done it right then; I could have busted his arm.

But I didn't. Instead, I shoved him away, hoping he'd get the point.

And as I turned around, I heard Dean shouting to me, "Duck Corey. Look out!"

I couldn't see Barker coming up alongside but I could feel him there ready to demolish me. I started to duck as Dean suggested but I was too slow. And then it became all to clear to me that I wasn't the only one here who had at least one martial arts move.

Barker kicked his foot high into the air like a kick-boxer and his foot caught me square in the jaw. I felt the pain shoot through my face and right into my brain. The kick sent me spinning backwards and I had to roll with it onto the pavement until I could get myself steady.

Dean was still hunched over, trying to get his nose to stop bleeding. His eye was almost swollen shut. And Barker, with Vic right behind him, was coming at me again. He had that mad look in his eyes like Arnold Schwarzenegger in *Terminator 2*.

I stood up. I cursed silently, wondering why I hadn't finished with Vic and then gone on to bust Barker's arm. Too late to think about regrets. Barker let out a maniac yell, made a charge at me, and then kicked out his foot again, straight for my face.

But I guess he was as much an amateur at this kind of fighting as I was because I didn't have to get out of the way this time. I grabbed onto the foot and yanked it higher into the air. You can use your opponent's strength to work against him, I remembered hearing Reeds tell me. I held onto John's foot and raised his leg as high into the air as I could.

He was off balance and fell to the ground. Unfortunately for him, he landed head first. I heard his skull connect hard with the pavement.

Barker rolled a bit to one side and then just lay there all too quiet. Vic looked at me and then at Dean who was now on his feet. He looked scared.

But I doubt that he was as scared as me right then because the sound of Barker's skull hitting the asphalt had shot right through me. I was afraid that I had really done some awful damage. Already I was silently cursing, I didn't want to get into this, dammit, as I knelt down to get a look at John.

I was afraid to move him. I had to put my face down close to his and I could tell he was breathing but I didn't know if he had just bumped his head or broken his neck.

"Leave him alone!" Vic screamed at me. I guess he thought I was gonna do more damage. Maybe he was thinking about himself, that he wouldn't have stopped, that he would have kept pounding a man who was down. But I had no intention of trying to make things any worse.

I watched out of the corner of my eye as Vic ran off towards the front of the school.

"What are we going to do?" I asked Dean whose nose was still spilling out his blood. "We can't move him. We have to get some help."

"He deserved it," Dean said.

"No, he didn't," I said, feeling guilty. "He's hurt bad."

"You gotta get out of here, Corey. Whatever happens, they're gonna crucify you, man."

"I know," I said but I still couldn't make myself leave. "Stay here. I'm gonna go inside and get some help."

But as I stood up over Barker, I saw Hartman rounding the corner of the building. Vic was beside him, pointing towards us.

I wasn't planning on going anywhere. I wanted to see this thing through. I wanted to make sure that Barker was okay and I wanted to make sure Hartman heard the truth.

Just then I heard Hartman scream something at me at the top of his lungs. I'm not even sure I really heard it. Maybe it was just a lot of garbled angry noise … but Heartless was mad and what I thought I heard him say was, "Corey, you black son of a bitch!"

Whatever it was I heard, Dean heard it too, because he gave me a push. "Get out of here, Corey. Run." And he gave me a push. And this time I ran. I saw that look in Hartman's face and I just had to get away from there as fast as my feet could carry me.

Chapter Eighteen

On the Run

I went home right away and all I did was sit down at the kitchen table and shake. I could not begin to make my brain work right and it was hard for my eyes to focus. I went up to my room and put on my stereo at full blast. I lay there on the bed trying to drive the craziness out of me. I stayed there without moving for maybe half an hour, until the tape ran out, but I didn't seem to have the energy to get up and turn it over.

Then the phone rang. I knew for certain it was bad news. I let it ring four times and was going to ignore it altogether but suddenly I became real curious. Maybe it was someone calling me to say that John was okay, that things weren't as bad as they seemed. I decided I should answer it.

"Hello?"

"Hello. It's the Dartmouth Police calling. Who am I speaking to?" It was a woman's voice on the other end.

I held my breath for a second. I almost answered the question but stopped myself as I felt panic sink into my bones. I slammed down the receiver.

The blood drained out of my face. Heartless had told them I was responsible for the fight. I was already presumed to be guilty. Man, what could I do?

I tried to think but my brain was like a TV set with nothing but snow and static. How bad was John hurt, anyway? I desperately wanted some news but I didn't dare phone anyone. Maybe Dean was already arrested. Hartman probably believed everything Vic had said. Vic and Barker were both considered "respectable" by Hartman because they were jocks — sports heroes … and because they were white.

The phone started ringing again. I didn't dare take another chance. I grabbed my coat and ran for the door. At first, I didn't have the slightest notion where I was going, but by the time I reached the bus stop and counted the change in my pocket, I knew exactly where I was headed.

Chapter Nineteen

A Million Miles from Home

On the bus, I had this feeling that everyone was looking at me. Man, I was feeling paranoid. I expected at any minute a cop car would stop the bus and then arrest me at gunpoint. My knees were shaking and I couldn't make them quit. I guess I kept my eyes closed half the way there, although I could tell when we stopped at the toll booth and then went over the bridge. A few minutes later I was off the bus and knocking at Larry's door.

"It's not locked," he yelled from inside.

I walked in. There was Larry, sitting like he always was at the beat-up kitchen table. The radio was on. He had a hand-rolled cigarette in one hand and a cup of tea in front of him. He coughed long and loud and waved the smoke away from the air in front of him before he could talk.

I walked to the radio, turned it off and sat down. "I got myself into a mess of trouble," I told him.

"I knew that as soon as you walked in the door. But don't worry. I guess you came to the right place. Trouble been looking for me all my life. Tell me about it."

So I started to tell him the whole story. Midway through it, though, the lady upstairs started singing and I stopped to listen.

"Go on," Larry said. "Finish it. Can't leave a man hanging in mid-air. I can hear her any time." He started to roll another cigarette but stopped, unrolled it and brushed the tobacco back into the little plastic pouch. I told him the rest of the story and then slumped back in the chair.

"Ain't nobody gonna bother you here, son," he said looking like he felt more sorry for me than for a boy who had just seen his dog get run over by a garbage truck.

"What am I gonna do?" I asked.

At first he said nothing. We let the sound of Irene's singing roll over us like a big bluesy wave of sadness.

"I'm gonna study on it," Larry said and got up to pour himself some more tea. He poured me a cup and set it in front of me even though he knew I didn't drink tea. "I don't have no Pepsi," he said.

I drank the tea. It was hot and bitter and somehow tasted just right.

Larry appeared to be deep in thought and he acted awful tired, like he was carrying around the weight of the world. He pointed to a little twelve-inch black-and-white TV in the room he called the sitting-room. I switched it on and watched a rerun of "Danger Bay" and the "Ghost Busters" cartoon. I couldn't pay much attention to the shows but I liked the noise. Larry hadn't come up with any real advice for me and I thought that maybe I'd have to leave. I was thinking seriously about running away from home and leaving everything behind. I knew that I could never convince Hartman that I wasn't the cause of the blow-up. It wouldn't matter what I said or what Dean said.

There was a knock at the door. I looked at Larry. He was sort of nodding off, still sitting in front of his tea at the kitchen table. I ran for the bathroom and closed the door. I leaned over the sink and thought I was gonna puke I was so scared. But I held a hand over my own mouth, knelt down on the floor behind the door and listened.

"I'm comin', I'm comin'," Larry said. "Hold onto your horses."

The door opened. Through the keyhole in the bathroom door I could see two Halifax cops. "We've been told that Corey Wheeler might be here."

"Who told you that?" Larry asked.

"We talked to his mother. She gave us your address. She said he might be here."

"I haven't seen him."

"He could be in big trouble. There might be criminal charges. If he's staying here, we could charge you with harbouring."

"Is that so? I didn't know that," Larry said in a non-committal way. "Don't worry, officer, I sure wouldn't want to get myself into any trouble. I never had any trouble with the law in my life."

I was beginning to freak because Larry was starting to sound like the old coward I had seen at the laundromat and at the tool and die shop. I was sucking in my breath, trying to get up my courage to go out there and face the music. No way did I want to get old Larry into hot water. But my legs were having a hard time getting me up on my feet. Then I heard this.

"Well, if you don't want any trouble, I'm sure you wouldn't mind if you let us in to look around."

"No, officer," Larry answered. "I wouldn't mind at all. That would be just fine … only I would like to look at the search warrant first. Wait now, let me get my glasses."

I didn't breathe. I jammed my eyeball up to the keyhole again.

Larry was shuffling around the room looking for his glasses. The policeman said, "That won't be necessary. We don't have a search warrant. The boy's just wanted for questioning." He seemed flustered. "But, if he shows up, you'd be doing him a favour if you told him to come see us or the Dartmouth police."

Larry had just found his glasses. "Yes, sir. I will do that. If I see the boy, I'll drive him there myself. He's a good young man and I don't want to see him messin' up his life. Good day."

The outer door closed. I heard the cops get into their car and pull off. I slumped down on the floor and started to cry.

When I came out of the bathroom, I found Larry making supper. "I hope you don't mind Italian food," he said. He was dropping long sticks of spaghetti into a big pot of boiling water.

"Sounds good," I said.

"Can you handle garlic? I like lots of garlic in the sauce."

"I love garlic," I said. "It's supposed to keep away vampires."

Larry smiled at that. "Vampires? I knew it must be good for something. My momma just always said it made you live longer. Maybe that's why you live longer, 'cause no vampires can get at you."

Right then I wanted to laugh but I was afraid I would start crying instead, so I just sat down at the table and waited to eat the most garlicky spaghetti that ever saw a dinner plate in the city of Halifax.

Afterwards I offered to do the dishes.

"Nope, " Larry said. "You can't do the dishes 'cause you need to get on the phone and tell your mother where you're at."

I didn't question him. I was wondering what my mother was thinking. The cops had talked to her and she must have been pretty worried if she was willing to give them Larry's address. The phone had just barely begun to ring when my old man answered. "Where are you?" he demanded.

"Can I talk to mom?"

"She's not here. She's at your school talking with the principal. What happened today, Corey? What's going on?"

"I can't explain now," I answered and I expected him to really go off the deep end. But he didn't.

"Corey, son, we're worried to death about you." This wasn't like my tough old man at all.

"I'm okay," I said. "I'm staying with a friend who's helping me sort this out. Tell mom not to worry. G'bye."

When I put the phone down I felt like I had just cut myself off from my home and my world. I felt like I was a million miles from there and wondered if I could ever find my way back.

Chapter Twenty

Confronting the Truth

Wake up," I heard someone say. At first I thought I was dreaming. I didn't recognize the voice. "Come on, son, wake up. We have to get going."

I discovered I was asleep on the chesterfield in Larry's sitting room. He was hovering over me holding out a cup of steaming tea.

Everything seemed out of focus and unreal. It took me a few minutes to piece together the events from yesterday and figure out why I was here. Then everything rushed back into my head all too clearly.

"Don't do any serious thinking until after you've had a good breakfast," Larry told me. He made me a big stack pancakes and made sure that I ate the whole pile. Then he handed me my coat.

"Where are we going?"

"We got work to do," he said.

I assumed that he was going to make his rounds and I was going along too. I was glad that he was trying to make everything seem normal. We drove across the harbour to Dartmouth and the fact of the matter didn't sink in until we turned down Lyle Street and were about a block from Thompson High. We passed a parked police car with two Dartmouth cops drinking coffee.

"What are you doing?" I yelled at him. "Are you crazy?" I wanted to leap out of the car and run. Larry had just turned in the driveway of the school. I quickly slumped down into the seat.

"Been a long time since I ever set foot on school property," Larry said, trying to ignore my panic. "I never did too well in school. Teachers always made me nervous."

Larry pulled his old clunker up right to the front steps of the school, turned off the ignition and pocketed the keys. "You got to go in and talk to that principal of yours, first thing. You tell him the truth."

"He won't believe me," I insisted. No way was I going in to give myself up to Heartless Hartman. "He hates my guts. The man has it in for me. I'm not going."

"You'd rather talk to the police first? It don't look like they're very far off."

"Why did you bring me here?" I demanded. "I thought I could trust you."

"You *can* trust me, Corey. That's why we're here. I can't let you go running off and ruining your life over nothing. You told me what happened and I believe you. Now you'll have to convince that man in there that you're not the one at fault. It's gonna be hard but it's necessary. It's very important to confront the thing that scares you the most. You can't turn your back on it or it'll haunt you the rest of your life. Now you get in there and talk to him."

I wasn't about to budge. I didn't know what to do. I looked towards the windows of the front office. The two secretaries were looking out the window at us. I'm sure they thought Larry's car looked pretty suspicious.

Larry was getting nervous, I know, because he pulled out some tobacco and tried to roll a cigarette but fumbled with it and spilled the tobacco all over himself. He gave up, crumpled up the paper and then began to cough like he was having a hard time breathing.

"Man, you need to see a doctor. That sounds bad," I said.

"I don't do any dealings with doctors. I told you that. Now stop trying to change the subject. We're gonna be walking through those doors in thirty seconds, or you're gonna be lookin' at one mean old man. Now move it, mister."

So I moved. Something had changed. Larry was going to go with me into Hartman's office.

The secretaries stared at us the whole way up the steps to the door.

"We need to see the principal," Larry said in a shaky voice as we walked into the front office.

"I'm not sure he's available," the one named Edna said, and she looked straight at me. She knew who I was. "Would you like to have a seat?"

Larry said nothing. We stood silently. I looked at the clock. 9:30. If life was normal, I'd be sitting in math class doing isosceles triangles or figuring out the square root of 4,598. The other secretary was on the phone. It was a trap. She was probably calling the police. I wanted out of there real bad and Larry could tell. He grabbed my arm and pinched hard into my wrist.

The door to Hartman's office opened. Heartless looked like a volcano about to erupt. "What are you doing here?" he snarled. "And who is this with you?"

"This is Larry Sloan," I said. I didn't know what would happen next.

Larry took off his old hat and said in quaky voice, "How do you do, sir?"

Heartless was baffled. He didn't know what to make of Larry. "Your grandfather?"

"No. My grandfather's brother. And a friend of mine."

"Can we have a word with you, sir?" Larry asked.

I think it was the submissive, polite way old Larry said it that defused Hartman. He didn't know what to make of the scene. Finally he said, "Come on in."

I could hear the two secretaries give a sigh of relief simultaneously. They had been holding their breath, not knowing what to expect.

Chapter Twenty-one

Back Over the Line

When we sat down, I started to try to explain. I wanted Hartman to see the chain of events the way I saw them. And I wanted him to know that I had been trying to refuse to get involved in a fight. I was so nervous, though, that it was all coming out wrong. My story was garbled and confused. And the more incoherent I became, the worse off things were. I just couldn't get the words to do what I wanted them too.

Then I realized that Hartman wasn't even listening. Right in the middle he cut in, "The police are looking for you, Wheeler. It's out of my hands now. I don't know what you think you were trying to do, but you sure caused one hell of a mess. Barker is still in the hospital. He had a serious concussion. His parents have laid charges and I think they did the right thing. You'll probably try to weasel out of this like all your other dirty deeds. But I know one thing. You are never coming back to this school. I'll see to that." His face was turning a bright red. It was clear that I brought out the worst in the man. It was hopeless.

I didn't turn away but looked him straight in the eyes as he shifted his glance from me to Larry and back. All at once it became clear. Guilty until proven innocent … only I wasn't ever going to have a chance to prove myself. What Hartman saw in front of him was a trouble-making young black kid who was no good and some old, feeble, good-for-nothing black relative. It wouldn't matter what I said or what the truth was. I was angry now and I was feeling beat. I suddenly understood what my grandfather must have felt and his father before him.

"If I were you, son," Hartman said to me, "I'd sit right there. I'll call the police and you can tell the story to them."

Heartless was standing up now and picking up the phone. I discovered that I was getting up on my feet as well. I was ready to run. I was fast, I figured. They'd never catch me. But Larry was quicker than the both of us.

He grabbed me by the wrist again and at the same time grabbed Hartman's hand, making him slam down the phone.

Larry was angry. I began to think he'd lost his mind as well. What was he doing? He was face to face with Hartman now and breathing like a steam engine about to bust. But in a calm, very quiet voice he said, "What we seem to have here is a communications problem. Maybe you both would kindly sit back in your seats so we can do a little communicating. After all, this here is a school and if you can't get people to talk the same language to each other inside a school, then I guess people ain't gonna be able to understand each other anywhere on the street."

Hartman had let go of the phone. Both of us sat back down.

"That's better," Larry said, still standing. "Now, let the boy start over again. Go ahead, Corey."

I guess I thought right then that maybe it wasn't hopeless after all. I took a deep breath and found that if I just looked down at the linoleum on the floor and pretended Heartless wasn't there, I could get it all out nice and clear. So I told him the story. I admitted to him that I threw the book and explained why but insisted that I had no intention of causing more trouble. In fact, I had tried to stop it.

"How do I know you're telling the truth?" Heartless asked. He sounded more reasonable now.

"I don't know," I admitted. "If you didn't want to believe Dean, why believe me? He and I are both the same, right? But what we told you is the truth. And you needed to hear it. Not some police officer who doesn't know anything about it. You know, Mr. Hartman, because you know we have one big problem in this school that comes from white kids hating black kids and us hating right back. That hate has been walking up and down these halls for a long time. You just haven't seen it. And now you're looking for a couple of kids to blame it on and hope it will go away." I stopped. I had already said too much.

"But why didn't you fight?" he asked. "Sounds like you had more reason to than anyone?"

Larry spoke up before I could. "Because, Mr. Hartman, this boy here is the grandson of Darlington Sloan of Africville who was maybe the second finest boxer next to George Dixon who ever came out of Halifax. And this boy here knows that with all that pent-up power he has inherited, that if he was to start poking a fist at people, white or black, that he'd maybe kill somebody and so that's why he didn't throw any punches."

Hartman was bug-eyed now at this revelation. And I was stunned. I wasn't a fighter. Never was and never would be. And I never had thought once about inheriting anything from my grandfather who I had barely known. But I suddenly felt a little larger, a little more powerful. What Larry had said now made me feel downright proud of who I was and where I had come from.

Hartman just shook his head. I was sure that Larry had pushed some magic button inside the man's brain and that Hartman was convinced I was telling the truth. I saw light at the end of this long, dark tunnel. Hartman got up and walked to the window where he fiddled with the shade. "Mr. Wheeler, where are you supposed to be right now?"

"Munson's math class," I said, thinking that this whole terrible bad dream was almost over. I looked at Larry who was starting to break out into a smile.

Hartman punched the intercom. "Edna, would you call up the Dartmouth police and ask them to send a man over here. We have two people here who have no right being on school grounds." And then Hartman looked square at me and said, "I don't think Mr. Munson will have to put up with you in his class any more."

Hartman turned to Larry. "I think you both better just sit there tight until an officer arrives." Hartman hadn't changed. His mind was closed. "Mr. Sloan, if you try to leave here with this boy, I expect you'll be in a bit of trouble yourself. So I wouldn't go anywhere." And Hartman left his office, closing his door behind him.

I looked at Larry. He was staring down at the floor in defeat and disbelief. Right then I felt more afraid for him than I did for myself. It scared and hurt me to see him like that.

"Let's get out of here," I said as I helped Larry to his feet. We led a worried retreat from the school to the car. Nobody tried to stop us.

As we drove out the driveway and away from the school, there were no police in sight. We ended up driving around and around the streets of Dartmouth not talking much.

Finally Larry drove down my street and stopped in front of my house. "Get out, Corey," he said.

"I don't want to go home," I said. I was still thinking about running away. I could handle it. But I was still worried about Larry, too. What would he do if the cops tried to press charges on him? What crime had he committed? And how could he defend himself?

"Go on, son. Get in there."

"No," I said. "Just drive." But my mother was already opening the front door. My father was just inside, right behind her.

Larry got out, came around to my side of the car and opened the door. Together we walked up to the house.

My mother understood who I was with. She looked at me and nearly began to cry. "Thanks, Uncle Larry," she said in the softest voice imaginable and she put an arm around me.

My father was not quite so pleased to see me there on the front steps with Larry. He pushed past my mother and he glared at Larry. "How did you get involved in this?" he demanded.

Larry didn't answer the question. Instead, he told my father, "Corey's a good boy and I tried to help but there wasn't nothing I could do." He pointed a finger at my father just then. "What you have to do, sir, is take your son to the police station. You need to get him washed and get both of you dressed up and go down together." And then he repeated that last word. "Together. Leave your mother at home. You two go in and let Corey tell his story."

With that, Larry gave a final sad look at my mother like he was apologizing for something. He turned around and started to walk away.

As I walked into the house with my arms around both my parents, what Larry was saying began to sink in. He was trying to push me back over the line. I'd walk into the police station as a white boy with a white father.

Chapter Twenty-two

The "R" Word

Larry's right," my mother said. "You and your father have to go to the police station. They say that boy is still in the hospital with a bad head injury."

I wanted to run up to my room just then and hide under the covers, pretend I was just a little kid again and this was all some kind of a bad dream. But as I looked at my father, I realized that something was really unusual. I was all ready for him to start screaming and yelling at me. But he wasn't angry. He was worried.

"Hartman wouldn't believe me that I didn't start the fight," I said. "Why should the police?"

"Maybe they won't," my father said. "Things aren't always fair."

Boy, he sure said a mouthful, only I was surprised by the way he said it. It wasn't hard and cynical, the way my old man usually is about his job or about his boss or about taxes or something. This was different. "We're in it with you, Corey. The whole way."

At the Dartmouth police station I was treated well. No one tried to jump me with handcuffs or anything. I was sweating a bit and kind of nervous, I guess. My dad explained who we were to the guy at the desk. He looked at us like it wasn't any big deal, then told us to have a seat. I felt like I was just waiting in a dentist office or something.

After about five minutes a police woman came over to us. "I'm Constable March," she said and shook my father's hand. Then, turning to me, she said, "The officer assigned to your case isn't here right now but I'm going to take your statement. Come with me, please."

"I'd like my dad to come too," I said.

"Sure," she said. "No problem. This way." We followed her into a little room without windows and sat down at a table.

"You have the right to have a lawyer here with you, you know. We don't have to do this now."

I shook my head. "No, let's do this now. I don't want a lawyer."

"You mind if I tape this?" she asked, as polite as could be.

My dad looked a little nervous about this but I said, "Go ahead." I figured I didn't have anything to lose at this point. Either somebody would start to listen to the truth or they'd send me to jail. At least it was better than having to stare down Heartless Hartman again.

She clicked on the recorder and asked me what happened in the parking lot behind the school. I told the truth, the whole truth and nothing but the truth. But I did leave out mentioning anything about who was white and who was black. After I had come to the end of the story, my dad was looking at me with a weird sort of grin on his face that I couldn't figure out at first. He gave me a positive nod of his head and a thumbs-up. He *knew* I was telling the truth. "It's gonna be all right," he said.

"We'll be examining this case further. As you came in on your own with your father, I don't think bail will be necessary," the lady cop said. "But Corey, you'll need to be available for further questioning. The Barkers have pressed charges as you know and the school board is considering laying charges, too."

"That's ridiculous!" my father said, jumping to his feet.

"Just let me finish," the woman said coolly, looking down at a manila folder before her. "John Barker seems to be over the worst of it. He's conscious now and, according to the notes here, the doctors say his injury was the result of a fall to the pavement, not from a blow to the head. But, as you might guess, we have conflicting stories about what really happened there. We need to hear from Barker himself." Then, turning to my father, she said, "As the parent here, we'll be holding you responsible for your son until this is all cleared up."

"I understand," my father said.

Surprisingly, my old man seemed in a pretty good mood in the car. I guess he believed that everything was going to turn out okay, after expecting the worst. But I was haunted by something that was driving me crazy. Larry had been right.

At the police station, we had been treated with a kind of respect. Everyone was polite, everyone was nice. All that lady across the table had seen was a white middle-class father with his white son who had just got himself into a little fight. It was completely different from the scene with Hartman.

Later that night I got a phone call. It was after eleven o'clock when my mom yelled up to me and told me to come down to the phone. "Hello?" I asked in a groggy voice.

"Don't worry, jerk, I told Hartman and the cops that it wasn't your fault I had my brains rattled."

"Barker?" I asked.

"Yeah, but don't go getting any ideas. I still hate your guts."

I think I smiled just then because I knew he was okay and because I knew I could live with Barker hating my guts. Some things will never change. Some *people* will never change.

"I'm glad to hear you're all right," I said stupidly.

"Shove it," Barker said. "I just didn't want people to get the idea that you got a crack at me and punched my lights out. Man, I'd never be able to live with that and I hope you haven't been spreading any lies about what happened, scumbag."

What a guy, I was thinking. Barker was remaining true to form ... and it was working out for me instead of against me this time.

"You could have told them I did it," I said. "Vic already put the blame on me. So did Hartman. He's been trying to have me kicked out of school ... who knows, maybe even put me in jail or something."

"It's a pretty picture, I admit," Barker said, "but Vic is a jerk who will say anything anybody wants to hear and Hartman, well Hartman is like the king of the jerks, so there's no way I'm gonna make him happy by lying just so he can bust your buns."

"Thanks," I said.

I heard Barker groan as I said it. "Save it. Now you'll excuse me if I get off the phone before I puke." Barker hung up.

The next day my parents and I were invited into Hartman's office. I reluctantly agreed to go.

"I'm not sure I've treated you fairly," Hartman said flat out, looking me straight in the eye. "I want to apologize."

I said nothing. Just saying he was sorry didn't erase the memories of all the hassles he had created for me.

"We think the problem is bigger than just Corey," my mom said. "There are many different shades of racism."

Hartman appeared more than a little startled by her use of the "R" word. He took a deep breath. "I hear what you're saying and I guess I have to admit that we do have a problem here at Thompson. Corey tried to convince me of that but I wouldn't listen. But you have to understand, I can't change this school single-handedly. I need help from students and from teachers … and from parents."

"What can we do to help?" my father asked.

"Get involved," Hartman answered.

"You mean like Home and School meeting, that sort of thing?" my father asked.

"Sure," Hartman answered.

My mother looked sceptical.

"I wonder if that's really constructive," she said. "We need to get to the root of the problem and also get involved in the decision-making, so we can solve the problems before they get out of hand. Where's the real power?"

Hartman was taken aback by the question. "It sounds to me like you should be on the school board," he said in an offhand way.

"Yes, why don't you try to get on the school board," my father said. "You have two years of university behind you. You've read plenty of books. Maybe you should give it a try."

Something had happened to my father because of this whole thing. He had changed.

Hartman appeared more than a little surprised, and for once, he was struck dumb.

"They'll never elect a black woman," my mother said, after we got home.

"Maybe not, but you could try," my father told her. "You're a fighter, a real contender like your father. I think a lot of people might like to see the daughter of Darling Sloan on the school board."

When I went to bed that night, I thought about my mother being on the school board that employed Hartman and all the other teachers. Maybe she could help change the system.

At school I tried to keep a real low profile. I figured I better just try to buckle down and do my school work. I walked past Vic in the halls and he still had it in for me but I just kept on walking. After Barker came back, I tried to be friendly, but he just ignored me.

Dean and Harris were like gold because they were always near me trying to make sure I didn't get my butt in any trouble and that other kids didn't lay some sort of booby trap for me. Harris was hurting a little because Denise had dropped him and moved on to a new boyfriend who was in grade eleven.

I guess that the whole fight thing had set other kids thinking about problems at the school between the blacks and the whites. I don't think many of the teachers would have owned up to it, and, of course, Hartman couldn't see the real problem.

I was still trying to get a good grip on exactly who I was so I sure as heck wasn't going to get too vocal about it. Low profile, remember? That's when a bunch of white egghead dudes who had never talked to me before in my life came up and said there was an opening on the student council and would I take it.

It took me about one second to say, "No way, José." I wasn't about to sit around in school longer than I had to listening to a bunch of brainfreaks arguing about what kind of trash cans to buy for the parking lot. No way. I told them all to get lost, but afterwards I felt pretty good that they had asked me anyway.

Chapter Twenty-three

Driving Lesson

I guess it was real stupid of me, but I was very pre-occupied. I never called up Larry to thank him, to tell him that things were turning out okay. So when Saturday rolled around, I got up and told my parents I was going in to Halifax to see the old guy. I wanted to check up on Darrell and his compadres as well. My old man offered to drive but I said I wanted to take the bus.

The sun was bright. It felt good jogging to the bus stop with the blood pumping in my ears. As I sat in the bus I decided I liked having this second life in the city where I was connected into a scene with an old black dude who was my grandfather's brother and some crazy young punks who could dance and DJ and do nothing but talk trash all day.

About a block from Larry's house, I came across Darrell stapling some posters to telephone poles.

"What's happening?" I asked

Darrell smiled. "Good to see you man. Where you been?"

"I've been in and out of trouble."

"That's all right," Darrell said. "Especially the out part."

"What's this?" I asked, pointing to the poster which looked quite professional.

"Promotion man. Free publicity."

"Your specialty, right?" I gave the poster a once-over. It said something about Rattletrap, Reeds and Tin Man being called by some critics, "the excellent new razor edge of rap/reggae rejuvenation" and that they were about to perform at a local dance.

"Who's the critic?" I asked. It sounded like these guys had made the big time since I last walked these streets.

"Oh, he don't want to be mentioned by name. He's modest, you know."

I got the picture. "Yeah, I know. Hey, what happened with the party at Freddy Reacher's?"

"You didn't hear? Freddy got busted for dealing. He's in jail. So the party's off."

"How come he got busted? I thought you said everybody knew he was dealing and the cops wouldn't touch him."

"I don't know. Guess these things change."

"Too bad about the gig."

Darrell flicked a thumb at the poster. "No man, it turned out okay. We were pretty bummed out and, you know, looking to be nasty just 'cause we were feeling bad. So we planted ourselves in front of the library on Gottingen. You know, all those ladies with blue hair and tennis shoes comin' in and out? And we were there to kind of like liven up all that deadness."

"I should have been there to see it," I said.

"Yeah, I guess you should have. Because, at first, I figured those librarians would go and call the troops but instead this guy walks out and just stands there watching us."

"'What's your problem?' he asks, and I tell him about how they come and busted Freddy just about when we're ready to turn professional and do our first gig. 'Show me,' he says and we have to change the batteries in the blaster so we can do it real loud and let this bookreader see what real life he's been missing.

"Only thing is, as soon as we finish he says, 'You think you can do that inside or only out on the street?' 'What do you mean?' I say, and then he says that if we want to do a dance, we can use the auditorium inside. He says he'd provide the p.a. if we do the rest, including the publicity. So I tell him publicity is my middle name. 'How much you payin'?' Reeds asks, always worrying about where his next dollar is gonna slide from. This librarian dude just says we can keep half of what crawls in through the door. We say that's all right."

"Congratulations," I told him and slapped him five. "Catch you later. I need to go see Larry."

"Say hi to him for me. I ain't seen him for a while. That car ain't moved from that spot for a couple of days."

When I knocked on the door of Larry's apartment, I got no answer. I tried a few more times and still nothing. Then I went upstairs and found Irene. Her door was open and she was sitting at the kitchen table peeling potatoes and singing like she was in the first pew of church.

"Have you seen Larry?" I asked.

"Now that you mention it, I haven't seen him for a couple of days. Not a thing. I was meaning to check today to see if he was sick."

That was all I needed. I ran back downstairs and tried the door. It wasn't locked. I walked in. "Larry!" I called. Nothing. In a house like this, it only takes a couple of minutes to cover the entire place. I found him in bed. All of his clothes were on and he seemed asleep.

"Larry, man, are you okay?" I asked but he didn't answer.

I had this awful fear that I was talking to a dead man and I was about to crumple down on the floor and start bawling. But Irene was right behind me, and she rushed up to Larry, saying, "This don't look good."

As I got closer to Larry I noticed that he was breathing but it sounded raspy and hoarse and his chest heaved up and down like he was trying to cough but he couldn't even do that.

"This man is sick," Irene said, "He can't hardly breathe. Call a doctor or an ambulance or something."

But I guess Larry was alive enough to hear and start struggling. "No way," he groaned. "I ain't getting in no ambulance. No sir." And then he started coughing and gasping again and trying to get his breath only he couldn't seem to grab hold of any air.

"What are we gonna do?" Irene asked, looking at me like I was the one in charge.

"Where's he keep his keys?" I asked.

"I don't know. Look around."

I looked everywhere and I tried the pocket in Larry's pants but no luck. I asked him, "Where are your keys, Larry? Your car keys?" But he had drifted off into some sort of stupor and his breathing sounded even worse.

Damn. "Stay with him," I told Irene and I ran downstairs. Half a block away I found Darrell.

I grabbed his shoulder and twisted him around as he was stapling up another poster.

"Can you hotwire a car?" I asked

"Can a fish swim?" he answered me.

"Come on. We got to get Larry to the hospital."

"Hey, I can start it but I can't drive."

So that was when I had my first chance behind the wheel of a car. Darrell, Irene and I carried Larry downstairs, heaved all his vending machine supplies out on the street and laid him down in the back of the stationwagon. Darrell hotwired it in about two minutes flat and I found out which pedal was the brake and which one was the gas.

All three of us were squeezed in the front seat. and I do mean squeezed because Irene was one big woman. She was half-turned around and holding onto Larry's hand. The man was unconscious and when he said anything at all, he just said, "No, no. I ain't gonna be cut up by no doctor." So old Irene, she just began singing some church gospel song loud enough to drown out Larry's feeble complaints and just about break my ear drum.

I found out how to make people stay out of my way when going through a red light by blasting away on the horn and I might have broken a few other laws on the way but I knew the route down toward Dalhousie University and that got us pretty close to the hospital. Then I saw the sign that said, "Emergency Entrance." I pulled in, squealing some tires as I tried to slow down. Poor Irene let out one high note that just about busted through the windshield but we did come to a stop. I hammered the horn and two guys in white coats came out with a gurney. They bent over Larry's face and I heard one of them say, "He's not breathing." He immediately began mouth-to-mouth even as they started to roll him inside.

Irene held onto Larry's hand all the way in and Darrell and I just kind of sat down on the curb and looked at each other.

"It's my fault," I said. "Larry helped me out when I was scared and on the run. I should have been back there earlier to thank him."

Darrell hung his head down between his knees. "That man has loaned me money almost every time I asked. And I ain't paid him back one cent yet."

After sitting around feeling sorry for Larry and for ourselves, we decided to go in and find out the verdict. The lady at the desk said we had to wait and we waited, for hours, reading those stupid magazines in the lobby until I wanted to scream out loud.

Chapter Twenty-four

Mirror, Mirror ...

It was night and I was ready to fall asleep when a doctor touched me on the shoulder. "You can go see him now," he said. "This way." I punchéd Darrell awake and we followed the doctor down one long hall after another until we came to a room with a whole line of beds and a sheet curtain surrounding each one.

There was Irene sitting on a vinyl chair asleep and poor old Larry lying in bed looking about as dead as any man I'd ever seen. He had tubes running up through his nose that were taped to his face and his skin was a funny, almost grey-brown colour.

"He's all right," the doctor said. "He's got emphysema. That poor old guy couldn't breathe. If you hadn't brought him in when you did, he wouldn't have made it. Somebody should have given that man treatment long before this."

And then he left us alone.

Darrell looked at Larry. "I promise to pay you back every cent," he said.

Larry fluttered his eyelashes and then opened one eye like he was peeking out to see if the world was still there.

"It's about time," he said in a weak voice, "but old debts always catch up with you." And he winked.

Then he focused on me standing there and smiled, "Corey, son, I always knew you could do anything you set your mind to. Just like your grandfather."

I knew exactly what he meant and he didn't say any more. I took his hand and told him to get some sleep. "I'll come back tomorrow," I said and turned to go.

Back in the waiting room, I phoned my parents and told them what happened. They came and picked me up. I introduced Darrell to them and we gave him a ride home.

I guess there's not too much more to tell. I went all alone to the dance at the library. Darrell, Reeds and Tin Man were more nervous than three blind mice chased by a cat. The place was packed and the cool had completely come off the crew. But after they made about every mistake in the book they sort of gave up trying to impress people and that's when they really started to cook. The DJ routines gave way to a couple of rap overdubs of instrumentals on tape and then when they started to dance on stage, the entire room began to come alive.

At their first break, I was still standing alone on the sidelines feeling more than ever like an outsider. I saw a few guys and whole bunch of girls crowding around Rattletrap, Reeds and Tin Man. But then Darrell busted out of the group, ran over and grabbed me. He pulled me back into the mob and made everyone shut up.

"I want to introduce you to my friend here," he said. "This is Corey Wheeler and he's the grandson of Darling Sloan."

A couple of the guys gave me a funny look, but I shrugged it off. But then some tall, wild-haired kid with dreadknots said, "All right," and slapped my hand. Darrell finished by saying, "Some people say that Darlington Sloan was maybe the second best boxer that ever came out of Halifax, but then a number of the critics believe that the man's talents were underestimated."

And when the cooler, calmer, more collected R,R and TM began to rap it out and rip it up even louder than in their first set, I asked a couple of different girls to dance with me and they didn't seem to mind. And as the music cooked on late into the night, I don't think anyone there cared any more what colour I seemed to be because with the lights down low and the distraction of all that flashy action on stage, it was hard to tell anyway. So I made this private little decision that what I would do was simply this. Every time I went past a mirror, I was going to look straight at myself, smile, and be perfectly happy with what I looked like and who I was. And I decided right then and there, as my feet were flying around on the dance floor of the library auditorium, that nothing was ever going to be easy. But that didn't worry me any more.

I thought about how Larry and I had come together and how I was able to help him out just like he had helped me on the bridge that day when I was so down and out. In my head, though, I heard that phrase Larry had used when things had gotten him down … *That's just the way things are.* And I knew that wouldn't be good enough any more.

As I looked at the girl who was dancing across from me, whose name I didn't even know yet, and as I felt the power of the music all around me, I knew that things *would* change. It wouldn't be easy. But the time had come—the right time, the right place.